THE LEGACY SERIES

SERIES TITLES

Burner and Other Stories
Katrina Denza

The Plan of Chicago
Barry Pearce

We Should Be Somewhere By Now
Stephen Tuttle

The Caged Man
Calvin Mills

A Day Doesn't Go By When I Don't Have Regrets
J. Malcolm Garcia

These Are My People
Steve Fox

Trust Issues
K.P. Davis

Adult Children
Laurence Klavan

Guardians & Saints
Diane Josefowicz

Western Terminus: Stories and A Novella
Michael Keefe

Like Human
Janet Goldberg

The Hopefuls
Elizabeth Oness

Never Stop Exiting
Michael Hopkins

Broken Heart Syndrome
Anne Colwell

What We Might Become
Sara Reish Desmond

The Silver State Stories
Michael Darcher

An Instinct for Movement
Michael Mattes

The Machine We Trust
Tim Conrad

Gridlock
Brett Biebel

Salt Folk
Ryan Habermeyer

The Commission of Inquiry
Patrick Nevins

Maximum Speed
Kevin Clouther

Reach Her in This Light
Jane Curtis

The Spirit in My Shoes
John Michael Cummings

The Effects of Urban Renewal on Mid-Century America and Other Crime Stories
Jeff Esterholm

What Makes You Think You're Supposed to Feel Better
Jody Hobbs Hesler

Fugitive Daydreams
Leah McCormack

Hoist House: A Novella & Stories
Jenny Robertson

Finding the Bones: Stories & A Novella
Nikki Kallio

Delightfully inventive and large of heart, *Burner* is a collection that reveals, and revels in, every facet of what it is to be human and fallible. Denza's characters fascinate for the simple reason that they are ourselves in every iteration. It is a debut full of grace, forgiveness, and startling beauty.

—LOUISE MARBURG
author of *You Have Reached Your Destination*

Katrina Denza's debut collection, *Burner and Other Stories*, is a powerful and moving portrait of relationships—warts, harsh words, divorce and all. You'll probably recognize these characters as your neighbors, friends, or family, going through the challenges of estrangement, loss and disappointment. As we all must, they find ways to cope and learn that life goes on. In a spare, compact style that has a knife's edge, Denza has given us a wonderful assemblage of stories that expose the complex underbelly of daily life.

—CLIFFORD GARSTANG
author of *The Last Bird of Paradise*

BURNER

AND OTHER STORIES

KATRINA DENZA

CORNERSTONE PRESS
UNIVERSITY OF WISCONSIN-STEVENS POINT

Cornerstone Press, Stevens Point, Wisconsin 54481
Copyright © 2025 Katrina Denza
www.uwsp.edu/cornerstone

Printed in the United States of America by
Point Print and Design Studio, Stevens Point, Wisconsin

Library of Congress Control Number: 2025943472
ISBN: 978-1-968148-12-6

This is a work of fiction. Names, characters, businesses, places, events, and incidents are either the products of the author's imagination or used in a fictitious manner. Any resemblance to actual persons, living or dead, or actual events is purely coincidental.

Cornerstone Press titles are produced in courses and internships offered by the Department of English at the University of Wisconsin–Stevens Point.

DIRECTOR & PUBLISHER
Dr. Ross K. Tangedal

EXECUTIVE EDITORS
Jeff Snowbarger, Freesia McKee

EDITORIAL DIRECTOR
Brett Hill

SENIOR EDITORS
Paige Biever, Eva Nielsen, Reilly Crous

PRESS STAFF
Karlie Harpold, Lilly Kulbeck, Kimberly Janesch, Samantha Bjork, Sophie McPherson, Madison Schultz, Autumn Vine

*For
Tom,
David,
and Alexander*

∞   STORIES   ∞

The point is not for women simply to take power out of men's hands, since that wouldn't change anything about the world. It's a question precisely of destroying that notion of power.

—Simone de Beauvoir

BURNER

There's a new chef at work. I feel his presence no matter where I am in the restaurant. I study his moods, the way his face looks at the beginning of a shift, like the surface of a lake on a windless day, and how it crumples and reddens with annoyance, glistening with sweat and topped by his chef hat—all lopsided and grimy—by the end of it. He's so hot that looking at him directly feels like burning my eyes in the sun, so I sneak furtive glances. The chef doesn't call out when an order's ready. He expects us to know the timing of things and we'd better not let a plate sit too long under the lamp or he'll whip it off the line and trash it right in front of us. A lot of chefs are yellers. The chef yells without saying a word. He can be humorless and rude, but I'm thrilled to be driving my Volvo to his house just the same. I have a thing for difficult men.

Earlier, at our staff meeting, the chef announced he had a full set of French china and asked was anyone interested? My hand rose, though I had no idea how much he was asking or what made French china any better than regular. I don't want the china. I want the new chef.

Following his truck through the narrow, tree-lined streets of suburban North Charlotte to his house, my heart pumps like a fist to the beat of a Drake song. We get out of our vehicles, and I pick my way behind him on the dark path to his front door. I follow him inside, squinting against the sudden brightness of an overhead light in the hall.

"Want a drink, Dimples?" he asks. My name is Erin, but the chef calls me Dimples. "A glass of wine or a beer?"

"Wine would be cool." I hate wine, but I'll drink anything if it means I can stay longer.

After he leaves for the kitchen, I set my bag on the coffee table and wander the shabby room. Above the baseboards, paint peels away in flakes. The furniture looks like it was rescued from a back road ditch. Built-in bookshelves flank the fireplace, empty save for a dozen cookbooks and a beat-up copy of *The Shining* lying on its side. On one of the dusty shelves, I write the night's special with my finger: lemon pepper veal cutlet.

I imagined more for him, imagined him living in some trendy loft downtown or an old farmhouse in the country, not in a spinster's brick ranch.

Cupboard doors bang and glass tings against glass. I head toward the ruckus. The chef leans over a cutting board in his kitchen, slicing and dicing. He's shed his chef-whites, revealing a fine, nicely muscled body. The kitchen is small and grungy. Some of the white paint has worn off the cabinets, exposing patches of ochre. The counter, a lackluster Formica. There's nothing on his white fridge but rust stains.

"Bathroom?"

He points a knife at the hallway.

"What are you making?" I ask.

"Nothing fancy," he says. "But we can't drink on an empty stomach."

"Okay, then." I head down the hall, hiding my grin.

I find the bathroom and pee. Naked cardboard is all that's left of the toilet paper roll, so I pull a packet of wipes from my bag. They're bad for sewer systems and I'm always afraid they'll clog the pipes but this situation is why I carry them. Also, they're good, in a pinch, for under the armpits and between the legs. The chef has a *lot* of hygiene products, which could mean he's uptight about bodily functions. I once had a boyfriend who wouldn't have sex unless hair was completely removed from our bodies. Jars of face creams, deodorant sprays, expensive-looking bottles of cologne, assorted hair gels, and a man-scaping kit cover the chef's bathroom countertop. In the cabinet behind the mirror: a tube of Tom's organic toothpaste and a bouquet of yellowed cotton swabs. I wash my hands with vetiver-scented soap. Squeezing toothpaste on my finger, I scrub my front teeth and tongue.

A bottle of pinot grigio, a pair of long-stemmed glasses, and a charcuterie board have been set out on a low coffee table near the living room sofa. I take a seat. I'm not hungry at all. At the end of my shift, I wolfed down my staff meal while folding napkins.

The chef sits, legs spread, on his L-shaped sectional. After pouring our wine he sniffs his armpit. "God, I need a shower."

How long should you know someone before you picture that person naked? I imagine soaping the chef's back, sliding my fingers over the span of his shoulders. I take a drink to keep my mouth from suggesting we go get wet.

"What a night," the chef says, leaning back with a sigh. "Busy as fuck." He cracks his neck to the right and to the left.

"Nice house," I say, trying to sound sincere.

"It's a rental. Furniture sucks, but it came with."

The chef's age is a mystery. I'm twenty-five and he looks to be at least a decade older, but maybe he just acts old. The chef before him was young and fun, always dancing to music none of us could hear because of the AirPods pinned in his ears. Charlie was his name. Every night he made us the featured special for staff meal so we could taste what we were selling. He was fired for using too many bottles of fine brandy in his dishes.

The new chef reminds me of my father, quiet and aloof. My father was a pilot for American Airlines so he was away a lot and only seemed to notice my existence if I was in trouble. "Your father wanted a boy," my mother once explained, though I can't recall the context.

"I hear you're writing a book," the chef says. "You any good?"

"I'd like to think so," I say. A creative writing professor once wrote *not everyone is meant to be a writer* at the top of one of my stories, a story that went on to be published in a respectable journal. I cut his words out and pinned them to my fridge with a Ruth Bader Ginsburg magnet. A reminder to persist.

"What's it about?" he asks around a hunk of cheese.

"It's about climate disaster and love and pain," I say. Actually, I write about assholes and the stupid women who put up with them.

He nods like he can relate. "Am I in it?"

"I don't even know you," I say, intentionally coy. In fact, a character much like the chef *has* snuck his way into my narrative, but he doesn't need to know this.

As we drink our wine and the chef chews on cubes of meat and cheese, he offers little nuggets about himself. He was raised in a small town north of Boston and went to the Culinary Institute of America. His family didn't have a lot of money but they didn't skimp on food. He's a perfectionist and cannot abide laziness. He has two brothers, both of whom served in the military. So far the only question he's asked *me* was about my book, which was a fishing question about himself.

"Have you ever been married?" I say.

The chef's expression grows dark. His knee jiggles up and down as he glances at his watch. "Shit, it's getting late," he growls. Every time he leans in to snag a piece of cheese, his knee touches mine and sends a shiver through my body. "All I can say is I hope you're a better writer than you are a waitress."

"I'm an excellent waitress." I am. Memory is my strong suit and I can be nauseatingly nice for tips.

"Not according to the customers."

"How would you know?"

"I've read the comments."

The restaurant keeps a basket of comment cards on the hostess stand. Sometimes a customer will drop his card in there rather than leave it with the bill. I usually pluck out the negative ones and throw them away.

"Ice queen, one of them said."

"*You* try dealing with the public."

"People love me," he says, a toothpick poking from between his beautiful lips. The chef has a nice mouth. "I feed them. I give them exactly what they want."

"Yeah, well, so do I."

The chef stands. "I gotta hit the hay."

I follow his lead, knees cracking, and grab my bag. My face is warm from the wine but I'm not even a little buzzed. There hasn't been enough time for that. I trip over my own feet as I move around the coffee table.

"That's what I'm talking about. Clumsy as fuck." He smirks at the scowl I throw him.

At work, the chef is graceful as he swirls pans, pours sauces, tames tiny fires, his expression focused, face red, muscled forearms sleek with sweat. When business is slow or my shift is winding down, I make up reasons to be in the kitchen.

"Shit, I almost forgot the china," he says.

"I could look at it another time," I offer, hoping for a reason to return.

"It's in the garage."

I follow him through his kitchen out to the garage which smells of motor oil and musty basements. The French china is packed away in boxes. He pulls newspaper from around one of the plates to reveal an elaborate garden scene trimmed in gold.

"A thousand for the whole set."

I look at him, appalled. "I'm a *waitress.*"

"I can take installments."

It dawns on me, looking at his smirk, that he's pulling my leg.

"It's not worth but four hundred," he says, grinning. "I'll take three."

I pull a couple of one-hundred-dollar bills from my wallet and hand them over. "Two."

He yanks open the garage door by hand and hauls the boxes, which I've been instructed to stack in his arms, to my car. I set them, one by one, in my trunk. We stand there, looking at a sky full of winking stars, both quiet, until I say, "Well, thanks for the wine and everything." I move in to kiss him but he shifts his face away. A dog barks in the distance, *Fool, fool, fool.*

"Let's not do that," he says, not unkindly. "We gotta work together, and…" He looks back up at the sky as if the words he's looking for are there. "Anyway, I like you but probably not like that."

"You're lying," I say. Let's call it a feeling I have based on the way he looks at me when he thinks I can't see him, or the fact that I'm the only one at the restaurant he's blessed with a nickname.

He scrapes his curls off his forehead, something he does when he's not wearing his chef hat or a bandana. "Maybe I am, but I'm tired as fuck and you should go before I say something bad."

He doesn't have to ask me twice. I get in my car and head for home, my trunk full of dishes I don't need or want.

Later that night, I lie in bed comfy in my oversized, smelly tee in need of a wash, and pull out the phone I bought at Best Buy with its pay-as-you-go plan. I scroll through my pictures and send the one of a crow mid-flight to the chef. I found his cell number written on the monthly schedule above the soup station, where all the staff numbers are.

He responds right away: *wrong # again.*

From this fake phone, I've sent the chef pictures of a toad's face, an overflowing garbage bin in back of T.J. Maxx, foam on my mocha latte, the scaly patch on the bottom of my left foot, and the end page of Anton Chekhov's story, "The Lady with the Dog."

I bought the fake phone back when I was trying to catch my ex sexting with other women. Maybe, through getting to know me—the fake-phone me—the chef will end up wanting the real me. At first, he didn't text back. After about the fifth photo, he wrote that he was sorry but the sender must have him confused with someone else. Then: *what the fuck are you up to?* Then: *are you on something?* Then simply: *wrong #*

Send me a picture, I reply now.

A while later, the burner phone buzzes. *U want to see my dick?*

Gross. No. Something arty

Three dots blink for a long time and I think he might actually be sending me a photo, but when his message arrives it's only: *fuck off*

Wednesday evening, a blanket of dark clouds threatens to whip up a storm. On my way inside the restaurant, the air plugs my ears, the kind of thick air from which a tornado can bloom. All the news stories of people killed in their sleep convince me it's not a matter of *if* but *when.* This is the kind of mess we've created with our gas hogs and fast fashion. The earth has had enough of our shit.

The restaurant is slow, only three reservations and no walk-ins, so Teddy sends our newest server home. Teddy's the head waiter and my best friend.

"I'm taking the ten-top," he says, sidling up to me at the wait station, bumping his hip against mine. Blond, long-lashed, slender with gym-pumped muscles, he looks like a model and he uses that to his advantage, charming everyone around him, including me. I adore him, even when the power of being in charge makes him insufferable like when, at the end of a long shift, he plants himself at the bar "working on the schedule" with an icy cocktail in front of him while the rest of us take care of the grunt work.

"Sorry to be pushy," he says, "but I need the money. I'm taking Enrique away for the weekend."

His mother sends him a monthly allowance and often drops off bags of groceries along with sale items from Neiman Marcus. I doubt he needs anything.

Teddy pours a fresh coffee and tears a sugar packet open with his teeth. His cologne has me in a chokehold. My eyes water.

"Too much," I say, waving the air in front of my face.

He presses his wrist to my nose, a classic Teddy move. "You love it."

Delilah, the new hostess, sashays in with a tray of clean candle holders.

Teddy looks up from his supply-check to tell her she's late.

"Stuck behind a train," Delilah says, an excuse she uses every time she's late which has been four times in the last week. Cool and lovely in her flowy black dress, mahogany hair waterfalling down her back, Delilah is so gorgeous, I can't help but stare at her. I wonder what it must feel like to be her, to move through the world with everyone's approval. When I was a kid, I used to look at random people and think, I could have been born with *her* life, or *his*. I spent hours on my thought experiments, convinced other people had it better.

By 9:00 I've only had a four-top and a deuce, so when Teddy's large table is finished, we clean up early. Delilah leaves first, then Bill, an older server with yellow teeth who has a habit of sharing too much of his personal life with his tables, and finally, Teddy.

The chef glances up when I walk into the kitchen with linens for the laundry bin. He's scraping the grill. "What'd you do? Chase everyone away?"

Like I haven't heard that one that a million times.

He tells the dishwasher to hit the lights on his way out. The kid turns off the machine, closes the lid then flicks the light switches. The back door springs shut behind him and the kitchen is suddenly dark.

"Hey," the chef says. The shape of him grows clearer as my eyes adjust. "How's my china?"

I haven't removed the dishes from my trunk.

"Fine," I tell him. The chef hasn't spoken to me since the night I bought them other than a snarky, "People aren't paying premium for lukewarm." He'd snarled it out to all of us, but his eyes were on me.

"You have panties on underneath that dress, Dimples?"

I'm wearing a black shift dress instead of my usual black pants and button-down. "What's it to you?" I say, both irritated and intrigued.

He slides his bandana off and wipes his forehead with it. His curls lie pasted to his head.

"Just curious."

The chef's face glows red in the light of the exit sign. The salty ocean smell of the night's lobster dish still lingers in the kitchen.

I grab my bag and head out the back door.

"Lift your dress, just for a second."

"You wish," I call back, giving him the finger.

I drive to a bar in the center of Uptown to meet Teddy and Enrique. I park and dig around in my bag for the burner phone. The picture I send the chef is of sunlight in the shape of a heart on the forest floor.

He responds immediately: *you gotta stop sending me pics.*

I send another. A close-up of frills on the backside of a shelf mushroom.

What's this

Guess

Not guessing too tired

I send a shot of an abandoned crab leg in the sand.

Who the fuck r u

Then: *U a woman*

I send him a picture of macaroni and cheese from a box.

That supposed to be edible?!

What do you know about food, I text.

Three dots blink and I wonder what he'll say in response, if he'll fess up to being a chef or if he'll send his usual fuck off but what comes instead is a list of his favorite dishes.

Teddy and his boyfriend Enrique sit at the short end of the long bar. They've saved a stool for me. I hail the bow-tied bartender and order a shot of Cuervo, which will last me an hour, at least, since I don't really like tequila, and listen to Teddy outline their November trip to Italy. Enrique sits on the other side of him, spearing the tiny onions from the bottom of Teddy's martini.

"You should come with us," Teddy says to me. Enrique nods in agreement. Clearly this is something they've discussed.

"You can even bring a plus one," Enrique says, an optimistic offer considering I'm not seeing anyone and both of them know it. Enrique's toothpick hovers over the last onion but Teddy gently swipes his hand away, saying, "Leave me *one*."

"It all sounds amazing," I say, "but I can't."

"Give us a reason," Teddy says. He leans in close and says quietly so only I can hear, "Don't say money because you can use my air miles and stay with us. We have a whole villa."

I would love to go, but it would feel weird tagging along unless I did bring a plus one and who would that be? The chef? In my fantasies he's a different, friendlier man, whipping up fancy dishes in my tiny kitchen that take hours to make, beef bourguignon or coq au vin, complaining about the lack of good pans and counter space. In my head, he's actually *into* me.

I had a roommate in college whose boyfriend took her on European backpacking trips, declaring his devotion in various countries by gifting her with trinkets and books of poetry and flower market bouquets. I've never received anything but convenience-store roses wrapped in cellophane and an occasional dinner out. Greg, my most recent ex, told me that I was slightly above average in looks but I gave a hella blowjob. He would say shit like that all the time, these non-compliment compliments. But he was a dishonest cheat. In the end, I didn't need the burner to catch him. He left his Samsung right there on the bathroom counter for me to read. I learned that he *loved* the red mole on Jill's back and that my nervous tics, like sniffing or scrunching my eyes, drove him nuts.

"Maybe I will go to Italy with you guys," I say to Teddy and Enrique. The three of us touch glasses in a hopeful toast.

It's Sunday evening, the only night of the week the restaurant is closed. Dinner is at my house. Angel hair with olive oil, parmesan, and chopped anchovies, a dish that got me through college. I'm not much of a cook, but luckily, most nights the restaurant feeds me. Teddy's brought a loaf of Italian bakery bread, which he's now slicing, and a bottle of Prosecco. Teddy and I usually take turns cooking for each other on our night off. Enrique sometimes joins us but he works for a charter airline and today, he's on a flight to Angola.

We take our pasta and wine outside to the narrow iron balcony, just large enough for a café table and three chairs. The balcony is the best feature of my apartment which is small and weird with its long galley kitchen and bedroom only big enough for a twin bed. The kitchen sink is in the bathroom which means that every time I scrub a dish, I have to walk a few steps back into the kitchen to place it in the drying rack. At least the living room is normal, with beautiful bookshelves and a fireplace.

The sky is a deepening blue, still rose-violet in the west. The couple in the building beside mine must be out because their lights are off. Sometimes, I'll sit out here in the dark and watch them, the man, bald and tall, and the woman, thin with hair cut like a boy's. They appear to be quiet and kind with each other. Their faces look serene when they talk or when they stand side by side in the kitchen chopping vegetables.

"New china?" Teddy asks, inspecting his plate.

"Yard sale," I tell him. The less he knows about it, the better.

"How's the book?" Teddy butters a slice of bread and passes it to me.

"I have this new character who's a jerk, based loosely on someone I know, of course, and the challenge is how to make them less of a jerk on the page."

"You're writing about the chef."

I consider lying. "How did you know?"

Teddy makes a face: eyebrows raised, squinted eyes. "I see you ogle that man when he's plating your food and you don't think anyone's watching. How quiet and tongue-tied you get around him." Teddy tops off our wine. "I don't see why. He's moody and old."

I watch a bat sweep the air for bugs.

"I don't know why you keep fixating on the wrong guys." There's an edge to Teddy's voice. Usually he teases me about my bad taste, but tonight he actually sounds mad. "Do you know how beautiful you are?"

There's a question. I have some attractive features; men have complimented my ass or my boobs. My face is nice—asymmetrical enough to be approachable—but guys don't mention my face.

"I think you crush on the wrong guys so you don't have to step up and have a real relationship," Teddy says.

"I feel seen," I say, not without sarcasm.

Teddy rolls his eyes then heads inside for more food. When he comes back, he mentions Italy again.

"I'd like to, but I don't want to ruin your romantic trip."

"You wouldn't be. It's not like it's our honeymoon." Teddy twirls pasta against his spoon. "Give him a sad backstory."

He catches the puzzled look on my face because he clarifies: "Your character. Every asshole needs a sad backstory."

I consider this. Sometimes the chef does look morose.

Later, I lie in bed with a moisturizing mask on my face and text the chef with my burner. *Tell me something sad that happened to you.*

He doesn't answer straight away so I watch *I am Love*, a movie I've seen five times.

Afterward, my mask washed off, I'm lying in bed, nearly asleep, when the burner vibrates on my nightstand.

You mean did my dog die or something

Anything

He takes so long to reply I almost drift off, but then:

My ex and me didn't work out. knew her since 4th grade

What happened?

That's it for story time. Send me a pic.

I send him a photo of a handwritten note I found on a table in a wine bar: *we are running out of time.*

Monday evening, I phone my mother, our usual time to talk, as Monday nights are slow at the restaurant and I'm home early enough to catch her before she goes to bed. My father refuses to have a cell phone, so I never call him.

"Hi, hon." My mother sounds tired.

"Is this a bad time?"

"Your father's laid up in bed at the moment," my mother says. "He's been keeping me busy."

"What happened?"

"A slipped disc."

My father is not an effusive person. He's only ever shown pride in me once, when the math department of my university asked me to consider changing my major. He carried on and on about that, lecturing me about building a future. To my father, math was smart, math skills were bankable skills. Writing might as well be tap-dancing.

My mother tells me she won the Mahjong championship for her league and how much she hates her book club's next pick. "Why do authors have to swear so much?" she says. "It's like they're *trying* to offend."

"Can I speak to Dad?"

Usually at the end of our calls, my mother will say, "Your father says hello," or "Your father sends his love." I suspect neither is true. But today I want to tell him I'm going to Italy. I want to ask him about his layovers in Rome when he flew internationally.

"Oh," my mother says, as if she hadn't considered I might want to talk to him directly. There's a clunk on the other end like she's set her cell phone down. I pick at the skin around my nail while I wait, but it's my mother's voice I hear next. "Your father's in the middle of an online chess game. He sends his love."

Teddy and Enrique host a party the week before our trip. "A small, casual affair," Enrique said, but when I pull up in front of their house, cars fill the circular driveway and line the edges of neighboring lawns. That the chef's truck is not among them is a relief and a disappointment.

Teddy lives rent-free in an updated bungalow, one of his mother's investment properties, and when Enrique's not flying overseas or staying in the Houston crash pad, he stays there too. The house has generous windows, modern, comfortable furniture, and pale greige wood floors.

The front door is open and jazz fills the yard. I don't like jazz—all those discordant notes give me a headache—but Teddy is obsessed with John Coltrane and Miles Davis. He always has one or the other playing in the background whenever I visit. Inside, a dozen or so people stand around the living room's flickering gas fireplace though it's 80 degrees outside.

Teddy walks up to me and kisses both cheeks like he's from France. One of his own cheeks is stained with someone's hot pink lipstick. "You look amazing. Bring that to Italia," he says, waving his fingers at my outfit. My bra top and high-waisted linen pants, both black, were scored from T.J. Maxx. One of three outfits for the trip, all of which I put on my Amex. "I have to mingle, but nibbles and drinks are all around," he says, before moving to greet a cluster of new arrivals near the front door.

The guests are not the usual restaurant workers and fitness people Teddy hangs with. In the kitchen, I pour sauvignon blanc into a clear plastic cup and take it over to a group standing in the dining room. Teddy's on the back deck, standing next to Enrique, pinching the cheek of a woman too old to be wearing pigtails. They all break out in laughter. The short, orange-haired woman beside me is going on about having given up drinking water from plastic because ocean life is dying, goddammit, and the other women nod their heads and talk about their hybrids and reusable canvas shopping bags.

After asking a woman in tiny shorts, her face aimed at her phone, how she knows Teddy and Enrique, and not getting anything more than a curt, *through a mutual friend*, I wander to the sunroom which overlooks the pool. It's the end of summer. Leaves and pine needles and dead insects float atop the water. I wonder how much longer before I can politely leave. The games will eventually come out—Teddy loves games—and the party will loosen up, but I don't want to stay.

I'm in the kitchen grabbing a handful of chips for the road when the chef walks in with Delilah. I turn my back to them and shove the chips in my mouth. Forgetting I'm wearing something nice, I wipe the grease from my fingers on my pants. I head for the guest bathroom upstairs to gather myself and wash my hands.

When I emerge, the chef's standing there.

"The one downstairs is tied up," he says.

"You followed me up here," I say, only half-joking.

He shrugs. His black tee fits nicely across his shoulders and biceps. "Maybe I did," he says, moving closer. He trails his finger across the bare patch of skin between my top and pants. "You look good. Come visit me later?" he says, grinning. "You remember where I live?"

"What about your date?"

"Delilah? I'm just her ride. Her car's in the shop." He nods as if confirming something in his mind. "You're jealous."

"Hardly."

He leans in and says into my ear, "See you later, Dimples. And eat something first. You'll need your energy."

"Maybe," I say, my voice non-committal, before heading down the stairs on shaky legs.

Five hours later, I'm at the chef's. His cool, crisp sheets smell of lavender. He turns on the overhead light when we first enter the room and I undress under an unforgiving glare all too aware of the rebellious parts of my body. I slide in between his sheets as quickly as I can.

"Slow down, slow down," he says, teasing. He undresses slowly, casually, like he knows he has a nice body.

"Let's get to the point," I say, the sheet pulled to my chin.

He switches off the overhead and sweeps the covers back, raising goosebumps on my arms. Then his mouth is on my body, gradually warming me up, area by area.

Afterward, we lie on top of the sheet, the blanket thrown off the bed. I'm so giddy, I feel like jumping up and clapping or yelling at the top of my lungs. Sex with the chef was so much better than I imagined.

"This can't be a regular thing," he says after a while, inhaling deeply, then blowing the air out in a puff. "I'm married."

"I don't see a wife," I say. Of course, I know he's talking about his ex, but he doesn't know I know.

"We're not together at the moment."

"Come to Italy with me and the guys."

"You're going too?" The chef groans. "That's all Teddy talks about lately."

"Think about it?"

"Nah, I gotta work, Dimples." He rolls over on his side and stares at me. His eyes are kind so I think he might say something nice, but instead he tells me he has to get up early so I should head home.

He groans as he leaves the bed and I get an eyeful of his glorious body. "I'll walk you to the door," he says.

We spend the first five days of our Italian trip in Rome where we see the Colosseum, the Trevi Fountain, and an underground crypt, damp and chilly and full of ghosts. Our guide for the crypt is straight out of a horror movie and Teddy has a great time imitating his raspy voice for the rest of the trip. "Follow me," he says, mimicking the guide's weirdly stiff walk. Our last day in Rome, we eat at a café with a view of the Spanish steps. A newly married couple, hands joined, stand at the top for pictures, she in white, he in a tux, onlookers on the steps below like supplicants. I imagine me and the chef in that scene, newly married, our lives full of possibility.

After Rome, Teddy rents a car and drives to the coast. He's driving too fast for the winding mountain roads and at first, Enrique snipes at him to slow down, then the complaints turn to pleas, and finally, tears. Teddy slows down and as soon as there's a place to stop, he pulls over.

"Get out of the car," Teddy says to Enrique. For a minute, I'm horrified, worried that Teddy will leave his partner, the man he loves, on the side of the road. Enrique climbs out of the tiny car and so does Teddy. Together, they walk a few feet away into ankle-high grass. Teddy leans his forehead against Enrique's and says something I can't hear. They hug. Teddy wipes under Enrique's eyes. When they get back in, Teddy says cheerfully, "No one's going to die today!" After that, he drives much, much slower.

Our first night in Positano, we have dinner at a café overlooking the pretty pastel buildings glowing in the setting sun. While Teddy and Enrique go to the edge to take selfies, a man sits in the chair next to me. "Hey," he says in a southern accent. "Couldn't help noticing you're all by yourself."

He's years older than I am, but he looks like a nice guy. Still, I'm irritated. He's not the chef.

"I'm here with friends."

"They look a little preoccupied, wouldn't you say?" His lips curl up in a sneer. "Can I get you a drink?"

"You know, you're right. At this moment, I am by myself." Teddy and Enrique are posing. Someone has offered to take pictures of the two of them. "And I prefer it that way."

The man gets up, seemingly unfazed, and wanders inside to the bar.

Later, when I'm back at the hotel, I text the chef from my burner. Instead of sending him weird pictures, I ask him if there's someone new in his life. In every place we've been I've imagined the chef by my side. I wonder how he'll describe me. If he'll mention my dimples or that I'm working on a book. I wait for his reply until I can't stay awake anymore, and in the morning, I'm crushed when I see his reply: *nope*.

It's the week before Christmas. The restaurant is packed. We're all hustling around, making mistakes, and dropping things. I'm working extra shifts to make up for the money I spent in Italy. I haven't talked to the chef, and he hasn't talked to me since I got back. I'm in the kitchen filling soup bowls for my four-top. My apron sparkles with glitter from an earlier table.

The chef snaps at his sous, "I told you to cut 'em smaller! Fuck!"

Teddy's next to me waiting for me to finish. "Someone's grumpy tonight," he sings under his breath.

"The fuck you daydreaming about, Dimples?"

The chef's face is red from steam rising from the pans. Bill is asking about his entrees, but the chef's ignoring him. He's waiting for me to take an appetizer out along with the soups and I'm not moving. I glare back at him.

Teddy takes his soup out. A couple of servers are at the fridge for the Caesar dressing. No one is talking. The fridge slams shut. All eyes are on me and the chef.

I pull my burner from my apron and send the chef a picture of the chandelier made of Capuchin monk bones, then one of the newly married couple at the top of the Spanish steps, and, finally, a selfie of me, Teddy and Enrique, sitting in the tiny, pink car, the sky a gumball blue in the background. Three loud dings break the silence. He walks to the other end of the kitchen to the counter where he keeps his phone. I wait until he picks it up before I text *Ciao.* I watch his face as it dawns on him that I am the one he's been texting with all this time. He glances back at me. I send another *ciao*, a word that means both hello and goodbye.

YOU COULD BE MY DAUGHTER

Before leaving for work, Charlotte sits at her kitchen counter and opens her iPad. She follows a variety of Instagram accounts: gardening, fashion, animals, cooking. Sometimes she checks her phone's tally of the hours spent scrolling through posts and reels and is horrified by the amount. Five or six hours in a day is enough to read a book, plant flowers in a themed garden, cook a gourmet meal and eat it, with plenty of time left to clean up. She's horrified, but the people behind these accounts help her forget she's divorced and living alone with a decrepit, ancient dog with bad breath, help her forget she is not the woman she was meant to be.

She's come to consider the people she follows, mostly women, as friends. Some even write back to her when she leaves comments. Her favorite is an Italian fashion influencer. The young woman's name is Vitorria, Via for short, and her long, caramel-blonde hair cascades down her back in ruffled waves. The week before last, Charlotte pulled out her wedding album and was pleased to see how much she looked like Via back then, over a decade ago when she was young and in love. The marriage didn't work out. The things she thought she wanted in a man—good looks, charm, confidence—turned out to be useless in a marriage. The way she and Trevor treated each other toward the end might have been funny had it not been so emotionally exhausting: Trevor kicking her in the shin one night in bed when he thought she was asleep or purposely leaving empty containers of her favorite snacks in the pantry, and Charlotte furiously scribbling complaints on index cards and pinning them to the fridge with magnets of places to which they'd never been. In her wedding pictures, Charlotte's hair was sun-lightened and much thicker and longer than now. Trevor used to wrap his fingers around it during sex and pull until her eyes watered. She hated it and told him so, but her feedback was pointless. During sex, he was the only person who mattered. He probably thought porn was some kind of instruction manual.

Via has posted pictures of her family vacation on Lake Como. It's afternoon in Italy, and the girl appears sunburnt. She poses with her new boyfriend, Giovanni. Charlotte's not a fan of the boyfriend who's covered in tattoos. He's a big-shot photographer, which is apparently how they met. Since they've been dating, Via's become almost skeletal. Charlotte wouldn't be surprised if heroin or cocaine were to blame and suspects the boyfriend is responsible. He has the kind of wiry body hard drugs bring on and there's something shifty in his eyes in close-ups. Trevor used to pester Charlotte about her weight, rubbing the mound of her stomach like she was pregnant, commenting on the skinny women he saw, saying how hot they were, and did she remember when she had a body like that? On the rare occasion he did the grocery shopping, he brought home low-fat milk and yogurt, knowing full well she preferred whole fat. All this while Trevor's own body had grown soft and larger. He was an accountant, and like Charlotte, worked in an office. She finally told him not to project his body-image issues onto her.

In these new lake pictures, Via's clavicle hangs below her neck, sharp-edged, and her ribs form a ladder of bones.

Charlotte comments on one of the pictures:

Your photos of the lake are magnificent. I've never been to Italy. My ex-husband didn't like to travel. Also, your recent weight loss is concerning! You're still beautiful, of course, but you look so much better with curves. Have you had a checkup recently? Is your boyfriend treating you right? xoxoxCharlotte

Charlotte considers herself a feminist and knows she shouldn't be commenting on this young woman's body, particularly in a negative way, but what if there's a problem? What if Via's boyfriend is emotionally abusive and harassing her about calories? What if she has an eating disorder? Charlotte scans the 520 other comments but no one else is saying the hard things. Other commenters tell Via she's beautiful and that she is a goddess.

Charlotte closes her iPad and scoots off the counter stool to change Stinky's water. Stinky is some sort of tiny terrier mix. He was Trevor's dog, but when Trevor moved out, he left him behind along with a half-dozen pair of stained underwear and T-shirts at the bottom of a hamper and a metal box full of tools Charlotte doesn't use. A week after he left, Trevor asked about the toolbox and feeling mean that day, she told him she hadn't seen it. She and Trevor live in the same small town, but they never run into each other. She doesn't hang out in bars playing darts and drinking draft beer, she doesn't eat out in the town's two buffet-style restaurants, because *gross*, and she shops at Whole Foods knowing Trevor prefers the cheap prices at Food Lion.

She calls to Stinky but there's no tap-tap of doggy nails on the oak floor. Hoping it will encourage him to eat, she mixes her leftover scrambled eggs with his dry food. Charlotte walks from room to room, searching under and behind furniture, but she's running late for work so eventually, she locks the front door and hopes for the best.

In her office, sticky notes cover part of her monitor. Charlotte keeps the books and answers the phone for a family-owned construction company. It's an exceedingly dull job, but her boss was willing to employ her despite her being fired as an interior designer by a mutual client. A spell of bad judgment was what Bruce, her boss, called it when he found out Charlotte had purchased items for her own house with the client's credit card. She doesn't know what came over her when she bought the six-thousand-dollar Italian leather sofa, a matching reading chaise, and the Grecian Marble table. She saw the pieces and was filled with a sudden and urgent lust for the whole display. She told herself she would set things right, that she wasn't really stealing as she had every intention of paying the client back, but the client—Buggy was her name—wasn't having any of it and that was the end of Charlotte's interior design business. The town was too small and Buggy had too many friends. In the end, Charlotte had to return the furniture which didn't really go with her tiny cottage-style house anyway.

Charlotte sets her purse in the desk's bottom drawer and switches her driving glasses for readers. The pink notes are reminders from her boss: swing by the bank earlier than Friday; call Bo's Plumbing for proof of insurance; Bruce's son will be in to move the file cabinet in front of the hole in the wall to block the mice; and lastly, one in neon yellow, telling her not to go on social media during work hours.

A sharp knock and her office door opens to reveal Jack Carrington, another local builder and her boss's best friend.

"Charlotte, lovely Charlotte, how goes it?" This is the way Jack always greets her and she likes it. She can be a feminist and still like compliments. Jack is an attractive man, broad-shouldered, work-built arms, but he's usually in a hurry so she doesn't know much about him.

"Bruce around?" Jack says.

"Is he ever? Did you get my email about the fundraiser?"

"I did indeed!" Jack leans over her desk and inhales deeply. "That is a lovely scent you have on."

"Shampoo," she says. "Make sure you RSVP."

"You ever been to Ry's Steakhouse?"

Charlotte shakes her head.

"You want to go Saturday night? With me?" He says this nonchalantly as if they're old friends.

"Yes," she says too quickly, surprising herself. Her underarms prickle.

"Damn," he says, grinning. "I thought you'd say no."

"You want me to say no?"

"Give me your address and I'll pick you up."

"I'll meet you there," she says. She'd feel better knowing she could leave anytime. Plus, you never know about men. "Six o'clock." She picks up a sticky note and starts dialing Bo's Plumbing before her face turns full-on pink. "I'll tell Bruce you were looking for him," she says, not giving Jack another glance.

When Charlotte gets home from work, she takes Stinky out for his business. She has no idea what he did with himself all day. His eggs were untouched, only a few kibbles gone from under them. Impossible to tell if he drank any water or if it evaporated. His bed was still clean from when she last gave it a vacuuming. She has no idea how many years—or more likely, months—he has left. She's certain he was heartbroken over Trevor's leaving. That makes one of them. A man who'd walk away from a dog he had for almost a decade and a half was not a man she wanted in her life.

After dinner—takeout from the local Italian restaurant she grabbed on the way home from work—Charlotte checks Instagram. A reply from Via: *Thank you for your comment! It's nice to know my followers care so much!* There's a rose emoji tacked on the end. Scrolling through Via's new posts, Charlotte stops at one of Via in a gauzy blue dress, her skinny figure clearly outlined by the setting sun. Her shady tattooed boyfriend stands next to her, a wide frog-grin on his face and a vape thingy in his hand.

Charlotte writes in the comments: *I hope you're not vaping, too. It's as bad as smoking and nicotine will ruin your skin faster than the sun. Also, your boyfriend looks like a thug. You can do better.* Not that Charlotte has done any better.

Charlotte started university when she was sixteen, courtesy of an IQ test that allowed her to skip seventh grade. She hadn't enjoyed high school much, tests were fine—solving problems and providing answers—it was the brain-numbing slog in between. What did she want to *do*, her parents asked her far too often at dinner. She wanted to do everything. The problem was in choosing. In college, she found philosophy through which the hues and meaning of language created ever more hues and meaning. She had a small group of friends who liked to micro-examine everything they were taught to believe.

One night at a local bar, after her roommate left with a guy she'd just met, Charlotte accepted the bartender's offer to walk her back to campus. "My little brother goes there," he said, though later she learned his brother had long since dropped out. "I'm Ted," he said, holding out his hand after drying it on the rag knotted around his belt loop.

Ted was nine years older than her. The age difference tricked her into thinking he was handsome. For their first date, he took her to an expensive restaurant the next town over. He made a big deal about her correct pronunciation of the word scallop. Most women he dated, he told her, said the word like it rhymed with gal. There was more than one correct way to say it, but she didn't want to embarrass him, so she kept quiet. Later, back at his apartment, the scallops she ate ended up in his toilet, while he kindly held her hair away from her face. She thought she might love him after that, but he wasn't serious about her. He liked to "keep his options open," he told her one night *after* she agreed to anal. The rest of the semester she felt disconnected from her physical self. Her classes consumed her. How she loved to puzzle out nuances of human thought! She gulped information as ravenously as she did food. Her roommate finally brought the obvious to light: *are you pregnant?*

Ted wasn't interested in marriage or being a father and it was too late for an abortion. Her parents convinced her adoption was the only option if she hoped to have any kind of future. "A mind like yours shouldn't be wasted," her mother insisted. "Plus think of the child. The child deserves more."

On the way to meet Jack at Ry's Steakhouse, Charlotte passes an accident. She tries not to look, but the chaos of the scene snares her: two cars, one more crunched than the other, two firetrucks, an ambulance, police cars, lights still whirling, and a woman sitting on the pavement, a limp child in her arms. Charlotte's mind goes to the child she gave up, as it often does. The child, the *girl*, could be a mother now, could be that very woman on the pavement, how would Charlotte ever know? A few years ago, Charlotte sent her spit away to Ancestry.com, her DNA a beacon, but she's heard nothing.

Jack is late. Charlotte studies the cocktail list and when the waiter arrives at her table, she orders a negroni because she's never had one and the picture Via recently posted of hers looked pretty.

The waiter delivers her drink and Charlotte takes a sip. Pleasantly bitter.

The couple at the next table are quietly fighting. The man shakes his head as if disgusted. "*Do you want to leave,*" he hisses. Such polite animosity. When Trevor was mad at her in public, he let her and everyone within hearing distance know it. Without being obvious about it, Charlotte eavesdrops. There's another woman involved. Isn't there usually? But by the way the man is talking, maybe the woman is a relative, his mother perhaps. The couple grows silent. Charlotte drinks her negroni too quickly and her forehead is gripped by brain-freeze.

When Jack shows up, her attention swivels from the couple to him.

"Sorry," he says, sitting down. "If you're looking for always punctual, you should know I'm not it."

"You know what they say about people who are always late," she says, not as a question.

"We're more creative and successful?"

"Attention seekers."

The couple get up in a flurry of huffs and scraped chairs. The man carries the woman's coat on his arm.

Jack fishes pink-framed readers from his front shirt pocket and picks up the leather-bound wine list. He winks at her. "Pink suits me, no?" And then, "It was either these or the leopard print."

The waiter arrives with Charlotte's second negroni and a basket of bread. She grabs a steaming hunk and starts buttering. "Bread is the remedy for drinking too fast," she says.

"Does your getting drunk mean I'll get lucky?"

"Oh," she says, unable to keep disappointment from her tone. She hears enough tired, not-funny jokes from all the subcontractors. "Are we going to do this? I mean, is this a friend-thing or a date? Because if it's the latter, you'll need to be more interesting."

"Ouch."

"Kidding, not kidding. Sorry, not sorry." She offers him a consolation smile.

They order steaks and salads and baked potatoes stuffed high with cheese and black olives. Jack's wearing a blue and white striped dress shirt, a silver chain around his neck, and blue jeans. She hasn't seen a man wear a chain around his neck in years, so retro, but it looks good on him. Now she wishes she put more effort into her own outfit which is only faded jeans and a black cotton blouse.

Throughout the meal, they talk about the growth in town, the fact that he's never married, and she mentions her divorce.

He tells her he knows already. Bruce filled him in. Things look up when he says he likes to read stories by Chekhov. Clearly, he's not stupid.

"You have kids?" he asks, stuffing his last forkful of cheesy potatoes into his mouth.

She tells him she does not. She does not tell him that she doesn't deserve to have them, that if she had a kid, she'd feel disloyal to the one she gave up. She also doesn't tell him, when the subject of university comes up, that she quit and never went back. Instead, she lets Jack do most of the talking.

Over their shared piece of chocolate cake, he tells her he loves to play tennis and that he belongs to a men's league in town. Also, he loves to cook and ride horses and likes to section-hike the Appalachian Trail whenever he can.

"Let's do Chapman's Knob this weekend," Jack suggests. "You like to hike, don't you?"

"Sure." She doesn't really, but she can do anything once.

"Great. Saturday morning. Wear bug spray and bring water."

They exchange cell phone numbers. When the check comes, he smiles at her with his eyes and says, "Mind if I get this one?"

On the way home, she catches herself humming though the radio is off. She feels generous toward the man who cuts her off before the light turns red. Passing by T.J. Maxx, she thinks she'll stop there for a couple of dresses next week. She'll need to start shaving again!

Unlocking her front door, Charlotte calls for Stinky. Usually, if she's out late, he camps out in the foyer near his pee pad.

"Stink?" she calls again to the silent house. She checks each room. She finds him in the bathroom, curled up on the floor of the shower, one of her house shoes under his chin as if brought in for comfort. There's a smear of runny dark shit on the floor in front of the sink.

"Stinky?" she whispers, though he's already gone.

Without thinking about it, she calls Jack. "What do I do with a dead dog?" she says when he answers.

"Is this a trick question?" His voice is warm. She likes the sound of it melting through the phone.

"No, I mean, do I bury him myself or take his body to be cremated?" she says, her voice shaky. "What would you do?"

"I'll be right over."

Before she can protest, he asks for her address.

When Jack arrives, he follows her into the bathroom and lifts Stinky's body. Her dog's eyes are open and his pink and black speckled tongue pokes out from between his yellowed teeth. She was never a dog person before Stinky. They were either too aggressive—jumping, barking, nipping with their teeth—or they were smelly and gross, their noses shoved into disgusting things. But she grew to love Stinky, the way he seemed to talk to her with his eyes, the fluff over them looking like brows, the soft, warm circle in her lap when she watched television. After they come in from burying him near the garden shed in the shaded corner of the backyard, they tackle cleaning the bathroom floor.

"I'm sorry the night ended this way," she says when Jack gets ready to leave.

"I'm sorry about your dog."

"He wasn't really mine. I mean, he was my husband's before he was mine. Still, I loved him. I'll miss him."

He walks over to her, draws her into his arms. "You want a happier ending to our night?" he asks into her ear.

She's emotionally exhausted, the high of their date and burying Stinky afterward a roller coaster. It feels good to be wanted, though, and he's attractive and kind. She nods into his solid, builder's arm.

They shower, and after, she leads him into her bedroom. A bedroom without any trace of Trevor, she made sure of that the minute the front door shut behind him. They lie on the bed, facing each other, both still damp from the shower.

His eyes are kind. She finds the weathered texture of his face sexy. Pressing the back of her hand lightly against his stubbled cheek, she smiles. He rises and positions himself over her, his knees, warm and hair-covered, press against the outside of her legs. He asks if she's sure, and she nods, her pulse rocketing against her neck. He moves down to bury his face between her thighs. She tenses, worried about the state of things down there. She stopped waxing after Trevor left as she'd only done it for him. It takes her a long time to orgasm and when she does, she allows herself to be loud about it. Jack slips inside her and their rhythm feels good. Afterward, she lays her head on Jack's chest, tracing the twirl of hair around his belly button, feeling the slowing of his heart against her ear, the ghost of him thrusting inside her.

"This was a hell of a first date," he says, breathing in deeply. His fingers comb her hair. When he moves out from under her, she wakes, briefly, then falls asleep again. She dreams of finding her daughter hidden inside a house in a different land.

The couple eager to adopt Charlotte's baby lived on a farm in upstate Maine, all the way up near the Canadian border, on the very edge of the country. Their lawyer told Charlotte the farm had dairy cows, a slew of goats, and laying hens. The house they lived in was old and rambling and needed work. They were both doctors, he, an optometrist, she, a family practitioner. He was on the town council. "These parents are a dream," the lawyer for the couple said. "You won't find anyone better."

She signed the three-page contract the lawyer pushed across his mahogany desk, her parents, silent pillars on either side of her. She read it before she signed. Some paragraphs she read twice. The document stated she was never to contact the adoptive parents, whose names were redacted anyway, and she was not allowed to see or hold the baby after birth.

As she read that part over, her hand rested on the mound of her stomach. The parents would pay for all prenatal visits and vitamins, and of course, the hospital costs. The couple's lawyer, a man with an inky mole under his eye, looked at her parents and not at her when he spoke.

After she gave birth, Charlotte was tucked away on the fifth floor of the hospital, two floors above her daughter and the rest of the maternity ward. The adoptive parents didn't want her to be tempted, her mother explained. "It's better this way," she said, setting a small stack of Charlotte's philosophy books on the stand next to her, books by Camus, Sartre, Wittgenstein. After her mother left, an older woman entered, asking Charlotte to give her baby a name. It was temporary, for legal purposes, the woman explained. Charlotte drew a blank.

"Anything, sweetie," the woman said, kindly.

"Persephone," Charlotte said, finally.

Her room was private and therefore, quiet. She drifted in and out of a slug-like sleep, a wide maxi pad between her legs. When she woke, it was dark. A nurse stood next to her bed.

"I can get her for you," the nurse said.

It took Charlotte a minute to understand what she meant.

"She's beautiful," the nurse said, her hand on Charlotte's wrist, checking her pulse. "You should see her. It would do your heart good."

"I'm not allowed to."

"Oh baby, I won't say a word. She's just so lovely."

Charlotte closed her eyes. Shook her head. She *wanted* to see her. But if she did, she wouldn't be able to let her go. The nurse left the room.

Sometimes, Charlotte replays that moment, imagining a different outcome. In her fantasy, she holds her baby, all those years ago, taking in her smell, looking into her eyes, feeling skin against skin, and walks right out of that hospital, her daughter held tight. She imagines teaching her about the frogs that turn to glass, the schools of luminous fish in the dark depths of the sea, about Chekhov and Camus and Schrödinger's cat.

Charlotte hasn't heard from Jack in over two weeks. She checks Instagram to distract her from the confusion and hurt she feels. Her house is too quiet without Stinky. Work keeps her busy for most of the day, but then she doom-scrolls and social-media surfs through the rest.

Via has posted pictures of her whirlwind tour of Rome courtesy of one of her beauty sponsors. Then there's couture week with its over-the-top fashion. Where would one wear a see-through dress with rhinestones? Via looks so thin she appears ill. In one of her videos, street photographers call to her to pose this way and that, lift her chin, put her arm on her hip. In all the posts, Via appears near death.

Charlotte comments on the most recent post in which Via is wearing a transparent, black chiffon dress.

Beautiful Via, please take better care of yourself. You're so thin it's alarming! Have I told you how much you remind me of myself when I was younger? You're much more beautiful, but my hair was the very length and color of yours. And we have a similar shape to our eyes. In fact, you could be my daughter. Sometimes, it feels as if you are. When I was your age, I had to give my daughter away. I hope she has a life as lovely as yours. I hope she's happy. Strangely, your posts give me hope that she is.

The next morning, there's a reply to Charlotte's comment: *Thank you for your comments! It's nice to know my followers care so much!* Followed by another rose emoji.

Jack calls one night when Charlotte is in bed, her face tingling and white with a moisturizing mask, but she doesn't hear it. Her ringer is off, and her phone is nested in her underwear drawer. She's trying to break her habit of checking social media. At work, she eats a peanut M&M every hour that goes by she doesn't look at Instagram. At home, she keeps busy with cleaning and working in the yard.

Charlotte is grubby from planting herbs when Jack's truck pulls into her driveway a couple days later. She brushes hair out of her eyes with the back of her wrist. Offers a half-hearted wave.

"Hey," he says, striding over to where she's kneeling. "I'm sorry I haven't been in touch until a couple of days ago. My mother fell in her bathroom. I flew up to Michigan to help. She's okay, blood pressure meds needed adjusting, but she kept me busy."

"Oh."

"I should've called sooner."

"Yes, probably."

"I hope to make it up to you. I got something for you," he says, grinning. She still doesn't understand why he didn't call or text sooner, but she likes the warmth in his eyes when he smiles. "You can say no, of course, but you have to come see."

She sheds her garden gloves and follows him to his truck. It's early evening. The bats have started their swooping and smells of neighborhood cooking hang in the air. Jack opens the passenger door. On the seat, a black crate with a wiggling, yipping thing inside.

"They don't have many of these little guys at the shelter," he says, pulling the pup from the crate. "They're usually the first to go. When I saw this guy, it was meant to be." The puppy is caramel-colored, with fluffy fur. She doesn't know enough about dogs to know the breed. She wasn't planning to get another one so soon, maybe not at all, but this one sure is cute.

Jack holds the creature close to her face. The puppy looks at her with his brown eyes, his whole hind end wagging. She takes him from Jack. Holds him first to her nose, then to her chest. Takes in the smell of kennel on his fur, his puppy breath, the tapping of his tiny heart against her hand.

Jack's excitement lights his whole face. She kisses the top of the puppy's head and looks into Jack's gray, smiling eyes. "You'll have to help me come up with a name," she says.

HERE IN THE JUNGLE

Stephen stands on Gillian's porch, hands stuffed in his pockets to keep warm, while she hassles him about this last-minute favor. He's asked her to keep the boys his week because he's flying to Peru with his girlfriend, Riley. Gillian is his ex-wife and Stephen fully owns the fact that he is the one who messed up their marriage.

"You're taking your girlfriend on a work trip?" Her resentment is obvious. As one of the chief operating officers of Canopy View, a worldwide zipline company, he's flown a couple of times with the inspection team to the company's park located outside Lima. She wanted to go with him, but knowing how the team was on these trips, raucous and drunk in the evenings, enough so that Stephen had to supervise them like a frat house dad, he couldn't reconcile bringing her along.

"The other way around," he says, impatiently. "This is her trip."

When he first started dating Riley, he was thrilled by the notion Gillian might be jealous. After a while, he figured out it didn't matter. He could've been fucking Angelina Jolie and Gillian would've been unfazed.

"This will cost you," Gillian says, tucking her hair behind her ear. Her hair is longer now that they've been apart. Out here in the daylight, he can see she's added red and blonde streaks into the brown. When they first got together, she had long hair and then she hacked it all off into a bob after she had James, their second. Stephen didn't say anything about it at the time. He may have been sleep-deprived, but he wasn't stupid. His opinion came spilling out in an argument a few months before she asked him to move out. He thought she looked like every other mom in their kids' school, consumed with PTA meetings and test scores and bake sales, and he'd told her so. He wished he had been more truthful: she looked hot no matter what she did with her hair. Anyway, he knows she's bluffing about it costing him as she's usually asking to take the boys extra weekends.

"Can I at least come in to say good night to the guys? It's cold out here." As if to underscore his point, the sky starts spitting out snowflakes.

"They're not here," she says, giving him an apologetic smile. "They're each with friends."

"How's things with Mr. Porsche?" As soon as he says it, he wishes he could take it back. She dates a guy who's practically retirement age, though considering what he does for a living, making money from money, he might as well be retired. The guy works from home, drives a two hundred thousand dollar car, and takes her to various islands for long weekends.

"Fine," she says, frowning. "Not really your business, though."

"You're right," he says, holding his hands up in surrender. "Tell the boys I'm sorry I missed them." Stephen's exasperation puffs from his mouth, a visible cloud in the cold air. He turns to step from the porch.

"Stephen?"

He stops. Looks back at Gillian. One of her hands, still tanned from the last island trip, rests on the door frame.

"Make sure your girlfriend doesn't post any more pictures of our boys on social media."

"Riley?"

"Is there more than one?" She smirks at him, playfully.

"That was just the one time," he says. "They're like two little dots on the beach. You can't even tell who they are."

"No pictures."

He clomps down the stairs. The snow is falling earnestly now. "No pictures," he calls back.

Stephen didn't know anything about their accommodations beforehand. "Somewhere in the middle of the jungle, but don't worry, it'll have everything we need," Riley said. Now that they've arrived, it's obvious they won't be staying in a five-star resort. Healing Way Center is a cluster of primitive buildings: a large octagonal thatch-roofed hut surrounded by smaller buildings of the same design, all on stilts. He's here because of Riley and she's here for her followers, to show them what these magical plant-medicine places are like. To invite them to experience one with her.

Riley is an Instagram celebrity and YouTuber. Her channel is all about beauty and health and lifestyle choices. Stephen has never actually watched one of her videos all the way through. Vlogger Riley is not as sexy as real-life Riley. On camera, she's prissy and calls her followers Lovelies and Beauties, and her voice, peppered with giggles and *ums*, is nearly an octave higher. It disturbs him to see how different she is on social media. However, Vlogger Riley is paying for everything, including Stephen's stay. Sure, she'll be putting him to work, but all he has to do is follow along behind her, documenting everything she does and says for her followers. Her phone would do, she told him when he said he didn't know much about cameras. Shamans and plant medicines don't interest him—he thinks it's all a little woo-woo—but he'd be a fool to turn down a week of vacation sex and maybe a fishing expedition or two.

They're greeted by the founder and director of the place, Dr. Eric Van Martin, a muscular, big-boned, bald man. "Call me Eric," Van Martin says, shaking hands. Stephen sizes him up, figures him for somewhere between thirty and forty, strong, athletic. Eric helps Riley with her bags and leads them to their hut.

"Dinner will be in a couple of hours, so relax, have a rest until then," Eric says. "Water and juice are in the mini-fridge. There's a guide and map of the property on the desk and if you want to cool off, there's a man-made salt-water pool behind the sleeping huts. It gets warm here in the jungle." He slips a bandana from his pocket and wipes his neck and the top of his head.

After the director leaves, Stephen scans the room hoping to find temperature controls, but the window screens provide the only air-conditioning. Patches of sweat pin Stephen's shirt to his chest. Even his balls feel damp and uncomfortable. He'd forgotten how humid Peru can be. Still, after the long plane ride and the boat paddled by a local woman and her scrawny, bare-chested son over a murky river hiding god-knows-what in its depths, the bed, covered in a white spread, looks like a grand idea. He toes off his shoes and moves the mosquito netting aside.

"Gross," Riley says, removing her clothes and bags of toiletries from her suitcase. "At least shower first before you lie on our bed."

Stephen lifts his head gives her a mock-sexy look. "You want to fuck?" He asks her this knowing she will not. She likes to have sex once in the evening, precisely at bedtime, and only after the two of them are clean from the shower. "I'll shower for a fuck."

Riley undresses. "You know when I like to do it, baby," she says sweetly. "But you do look cute under that netting. Come rinse off with me instead."

With great effort, Stephen heaves his hot, tired body from the bed, dropping a trail of smelly clothes behind him. He follows her pert little ass into the teak-covered bathroom. There's a view of the jungle out the floor-to-ceiling window.

"You are going to love this place," Riley says, pouring eucalyptus-scented shampoo into her palm. Riley is a knockout. Not that Gillian isn't beautiful, but Riley is different-level-beautiful, a level he previously thought was off-limits. Her attachment to him, when she could have anyone, is inexplicable. They met at the veterinarian's office. Stephen brought his new puppy, Dillion, to have his shots and Riley was there with her French bulldog, Petunia. He hadn't had a dog since he was a kid. Gillian was allergic. The boys went nuts when they walked into his condo and saw the squiggling, squeaking ball of black and tan fur.

In the vet's waiting room, Riley sat across from him in her skin-tight jeans and low-cut black blouse, looking like a model, her face calm and relaxed, and he couldn't help but notice her among the other pet owners, cooing to their sick pets, anxiety pinching their faces. Out in the parking lot she gifted him with one of her dazzling smiles. They happened to be parked next to one another, and as Petunia went to town sniffing Dillion's butt, he and Riley got to talking about dogs in general, then their own, and after a few minutes *she* asked *him* to dinner at the new Michelin-starred place on the other side of the city.

Riley hands him her shower gel. "Wash my back?"

"Why do you love me, again?" Stephen asks.

"Because you're sweet and you make me laugh," she says. His hands glide the gel over her shoulder blades. He's a decade older than she and he has no idea if there's a future with her. The break with Gillian has taught him nothing is certain. But being around Riley makes him feel younger, maybe even less cynical. He's more patient with the boys, more relaxed in both his job and at home. Before he totally blew up his marriage, he'd felt good with Gillian, too, but he got lazy in the relationship. The kids brought new distractions and sapped his energy. With Riley, things are simpler. And she believes he's a nice guy.

"I can't wait for you to try plant medicine with me," she says, turning around and resting her hands on his shoulders. She moves out from under the showerhead and the water sprays his face.

"Yeah…not sure about that," Stephen says. He's not here to partake in any of what this place is selling. He was willing to come on this trip to help, but he's never even smoked pot. "Some of that shit is questionable."

"Plant allies have the potential to cure depression and basically any psychological issue way better than pharmaceuticals." She sounds like an ad.

"Let's fuck," he says, hopeful.

"I have too much to do," she says, "I need to make a post or two and I need to unpack."

Stephen soaps and rinses as he watches her leave the shower. "Come back," he mock-calls after her.

Meals are served family-style in the dining hall, which, unlike the rest of the buildings, is long and rectangular. Getting there from their sleeping hut is a short walk between the center's small patch of manicured lawn on one side, and the jungle leaning in on the other. Stephen visited the Peruvian jungle previously with Canopy View, though the zipline wasn't as *in the thick of it* as the company made it appear, and he and the team made sure not to venture too far away from their site as all manner of horrible things were hidden from view: pit vipers, anacondas, spiders, poisonous frogs, biting monkeys.

Inside the dining hall, Eric Van Martin sits at one end of a long table next to a young guy in a rainbow-colored knit cap. About a half-dozen men in tan shirts with the center's logo cluster together at the other end, talking and laughing. Eric waves, motioning for Stephen and Riley to join him.

Mike with the knit cap, Stephen learns, is from Indiana and he's writing a book. "Researching indigenous communities and their impact on the land," he tells them. Mike is baby-faced save for the dark bit of fuzz below his chin. He looks close to Riley's age. Mike removes his cap revealing matted dirty blond hair. "You into ayahuasca?" he asks Stephen.

"I'm a tag-along," Stephen says, surveying the array of food on the table. Riley had him prepare for the trip by eliminating toxins the week before. No steak, no soda, no alcohol. He managed to sneak in a couple of burgers, but for the most part, he stuck to it. He wanted to be supportive. Now, he's ravenous and all he sees before him are bowls of vegetables and rice. He doesn't know why he thought the break from the good stuff would end once they got here, other than assuming a vacation is supposed to be fun.

Riley introduces herself. "I'm here to feature Eric's retreat on my YouTube platform," she says in her higher, made-for-social-media voice, dialing up her charm. "Maybe you've seen my channel?"

Stephen wonders in what universe does she think this dude watches beauty videos.

Mike grins. "Nah. I don't watch YouTube and I'm not on the socials."

Eric passes bowls of food around the table. He says something in Spanish to the workers at the end and they laugh.

"What inspired you to open this place," Stephen asks Eric. His plate is heaping with things he doesn't recognize. What he wants is a Porterhouse.

Eric gives a bitter smile. "I moved here to get away from all the crazy shit back in the states."

They all nod and Mike says, "There's no shortage of crazy shit anywhere."

Eric continues, "Yeah, for me it was med school, then full-on with my neurology practice. Hardly any time off and

I was becoming a real asshole. I booked a trip to the jungle to get myself right and never left."

"Lucky for us," Riley says, cheerfully. Mike looks over at Riley, throws her a smile. Stephen would bet money it's not her brain that's lighting up his face. "When can I start filming?" Riley asks Eric.

"Tomorrow. We'll go round to the massage and meditation hut, and from there, I'll show you a behind-the-scenes on how this place runs."

"Will I be able to show the ceremonies?"

"Off limits, I'm afraid. Privacy reasons." Eric pours lemon water into his glass then hands the pitcher to Mike. "But you're free to talk about your own experience."

"So, what do you do in the real world?" Mike asks Stephen.

"I run a zipline company," Stephen says. "This isn't my first time in Peru, actually. We have a site here."

Mike rolls his eyes. "Of course, you do."

"It's fun." Stephen laughs good-naturedly. "You ought to try it."

"The zipline connects people to the rainforest," Riley says defensively, squeezing Stephen's hand.

Mike scoffs and says to Stephen, "Is that what you tell yourself?"

"It actually does. And there's little to no impact on the environment," Stephen says.

"Except the trees you ruin. And how much awareness are people getting as they're zipping by too fast to notice anything but their own adrenaline rush?"

Stephen has never really thought about the company's impact beyond its marketing angle. Kind of like zoos: get people interested and they'll care. Stephen's job involves numbers, operations, strategies for growth, not ethical arguments. "I'm just the numbers guy," he says, finally.

"Hey, I don't mean to give you a hard time," Mike says. "I'm just the science guy." He winks at Riley.

If Stephen wasn't so tired from travel, he'd have a pithy comeback. Environmental issues aren't something he's put much thought into. Feeding his kids and paying for their education were more his concern.

The next night, after a full day of fresh fruit, grains, and weird yellow things that tasted almost like meat, a dip in the pool, and one of the best massages he's had in his life, Stephen follows Riley into the ceremonial hut. The previous night was a wash. Stephen was annoyed by having to defend his position to Mike. It made him look bad in front of Riley, even though she made it clear she was on Stephen's side. He went for a walk to calm down, to try to figure out why the conversation had gotten under his skin so easily, and by the time he came back, Riley was already asleep.

During his walk, Stephen kept thinking about what Gillian would've said about the guy: how self-important he was, how it's easy to have ideals when you don't have bills, etc. Gillian would've sliced through his sanctimonious bullshit. Stephen never enjoyed being the target of her sharp tongue, but he had an appreciation for it.

Tonight, ayahuasca. Against his better judgment, he's agreed to try it. He's not exactly looking forward to this experience, but it's important to Riley. Three medicine ceremonies over the course of a week, along with the massages, yoga, which he'll skip, meditation sessions, which he'll mostly sleep through, a couple of jungle treks, and a boat tour of the Amazon with the option to fish. Overall, not a bad way to spend a week.

The ceremonial hut is circular and smells of vegetation and something sweet and pungent. Mattresses circle the center like petals on a flower. They're all covered with faded patchwork quilts, a puke bucket next to each. Riley walks in behind him, filming her entrance and a view of the octagonal room. She waves to Stephen, aiming her phone's camera at him. Outside, various insects and frogs sound off.

"Take my picture, baby," Riley says, handing him her phone. She poses with her arms spread wide, the piercing on her belly button poking out between her top and her denim shorts, before claiming one of the mattresses. She pretends to throw up in the bucket. "We're not posting that one," she says, laughing. "Switch to video in a sec." She arranges her bangs to fall like curtains around her face. When she gives the okay, Stephen pushes record.

"Hello, lovelies," Riley says to the phone's camera. "Tonight's the first ceremony. I won't be able to film it while it's happening, but I will give you all a full update afterwards." She motions for him to pan the room, but it takes him a minute to understand what she's asking. "You'd make a lousy Instahusband," she teases after they finish. Unlike when he was dating Gillian, he doesn't feel the pull toward something more permanent with Riley. He cares about her, yes, and they have fun, despite her quirks and weird rules for sex. She's invited him to live with her in her apartment decorated with white furniture and pink and gold accent pieces, but he can't bring himself to do it, can't imagine their two dogs and his two kids all tumbling around in a place like that.

Eric enters the hut with the shaman, a thin white-haired man in a long, patterned poncho. The shaman takes a chair at the center of the room. A small wooden table next to him holds a variety of bowls and cups. Mike, knit cap atop his head, takes the mattress next to Riley. Eric asks Riley to turn her phone off.

The shaman gives a blessing to the ayahuasca with a series of chants and guttural singing. After, Eric passes a white cup to each of the participants. Sitting cross-legged on her mattress, Riley blows Stephen a kiss. She raises the cup to her mouth. He watches her face for a reaction, some indication it doesn't taste as bad as he suspects. Medicine always tastes like shit. She swallows, shivers, her mouth a grimace. He takes a cautious sip of the dark liquid. Thick on his tongue and dirty, like rancid, mildewed syrup. *Fuck it*, he thinks before downing the entire cup.

He's not sure how much time has passed. Riley's on her knees, swaying and hugging herself, smiling like she's remembering something pleasant. It feels like he drank a cup of mud and spaced out for a minute. No dramatic revelations, no hallucinations. Eric sits next to the shaman, looking calm and peaceful. Mike, on the other side of Riley, lies at the edge of his mattress, muttering to himself. The more Stephen focuses on the other people in the room, the stranger they seem. His heart picks up its pace, pulsing in his throat. Is it the cause of the sudden, sharp pain he feels in his chest? He closes his eyes and it's Gillian's face he sees. Her sweaty hair sticks to the sides of her face. She's holding Aaron, their firstborn, in the crook of her arm, preparing to nurse. Stephen cools her forehead while Gillian helps their son latch. The scene is dizzying and beautiful but doesn't last for long before he's thrust back into the present, thinking about how dry his tongue is. He opens his eyes. Mike is pale, his knit cap on the mattress next to him, his hair damp. Riley's still swaying and smiling. Eric's a stone, his face serene. The shaman looks over at Stephen and gives a subtle nod. Other than his dry mouth, he doesn't feel much different. At least he's not puking.

"Oh my god, lovelies! That was *so* intense!" Riley's talking into her phone, which she's set on a tripod back in their hut, her ring light lending her face a pretty glow. Stephen's still relaxing in bed. Riley, looking dazed and sexy, recaps her experience for her followers. Stephen hopes she makes it quick so they can fuck again. As soon as they got back from the ceremony, she was all over him. He was spreading Riley's legs to have a little taste, but to his surprise, it was

his ex-wife who came to mind, her and her sturdy, smooth-skinned legs. He remembered the time he and Gillian were in bed, both almost blue from the cold, and his frozen fingers on her thighs made her yelp. Earlier, he'd driven them into a snowbank one frigid February night on the way home from a gala. They had been fighting about what they seemed to always fight about, the boys, who were at that moment home with a sitter and were a handful at two and four, and the housework that Stephen didn't do, and how tired Gillian was of doing it all herself. All but make the money, he hadn't said, but he wanted to. The argument distracted him from spotting the patch of black ice and in a swerve and a spin, they were stuck.

"This is your fault," Gillian said. Her eyes looked dark and shiny in the moonlight. Anger radiated from her like heat.

Wanting the bickering to end, Stephen agreed with her. It was late and there was no traffic on the dark country road, and he couldn't get the car to budge. After thirty minutes stuck, the windows fogged from their breath, Gillian's teeth started crashing against each other. She wore an evening dress, heels, and a coat that was more for show than practical. He removed his own wool jacket and arranged it over her. He climbed out of the car into frigid air that chewed at his lungs and nostrils, and he hoofed it to the nearest house two miles up the road. His feet throbbed with pain. The guy who answered the door was glad to help push the car free and it wasn't long before he and Gillian were back on the road, then back home, laughing about the experience. She held him tightly that night in bed. He felt like a hero though he knew he wasn't.

In their hut, Riley fingers the length of her hair while she tells her followers about her experience. On camera she touches her hair to the point of distraction. He's thought about telling her, but she gets defensive and snippy if she feels criticized, so he'll let someone else tell her. Someone will. Someone always posts rude critical comments, some sexual, some just mean, and Stephen must remind her of how wonderful she is and that some people are assholes.

"Like, I must have been floating for hours," Riley says to her viewers, "like I was hanging in some ethereal, sparkly netting, and from where I was, I could see how all the things you think are separate are actually connected into one giant…I don't know, some organism-like thing." Riley looks at him and he nods, encouraging her to keep going. "Like, I was part of everything around me, all the color, the light, the shapes. It was all me. At one point, I was literally looking down at myself and thinking how strange and wonderful my body was. How, like, the sight of it and its weirdness was funny and touching at the same time."

Riley continues, though she's basically just babbling now. Stephen motions for her to join him on the bed. He wants to connect with her again. Wants to rid himself of residual longing for his ex.

Riley waves him away.

He pats the bed again.

She turns to face away from him, repositions her phone and light, and goes on talking to her fans.

An army of mosquitos pierces Stephen's face despite the layer of toxic bug spray he coated himself with. His feet, moist and hot inside his rubber waders, itch. Five people from the center have traveled by boat to a smaller tributary that delivered them to the path on which they're presently slogging: Eric, Riley, Mike, their short, overweight guide Juan, and Stephen. So far, Stephen hasn't seen a whole lot of wildlife, and he's totally okay with that, but Juan has promised they'll see something by the trek's end.

Riley's busy filming the entire expedition, chatting away to her legion of admirers, giving them something different from her usual Get Ready With Me and shopping haul videos. Mike is velcroed to her side, placing a hand on her elbow to guide her over roots in the path. Stephen finds Mike's gallantry irksome but sees no good way to intercede without appearing to be a jealous jerk, so he takes up the rear while Eric and Juan lead. Up ahead, Riley says something to make Mike laugh. Earlier, as they were starting out, Mike pointed out various plants, telling her about their special properties and Riley was oohing like she was impressed. Stephen doesn't like know-it-alls. Particularly those with eyes for his girlfriend.

Not that he can have much claim on her. He knows someday she'll move on to someone cooler, someone younger, with similar life goals. He and Gillian once shared similar goals: career, kids, nice house, summer vacations, retirement funds. He's not entirely sure what Riley's goals are other than to conquer the algorithm and increase her views. Riley and Gillian couldn't be more different. Gillian doesn't concern herself with makeup and serums. She's a little thicker around the middle after the kids, but he likes the mound of her stomach and her full ass. He likes that she's down-to-earth.

When he was with Gillian, he didn't feel self-conscious about the balding spot near the back of his head, or the paunch he'd developed. And even though Riley isn't mean-spirited when she teases him about needing to work out, it still pokes his pride a bit. Gillian felt like home to Stephen but she'd been clear from the start: infidelity was non-negotiable. She lived up to her word. He can't even recall the woman's name, only the fact she'd been seated next to him at a corporate dinner. Her dark brown hair was pulled up off her face and neck into a complicated hairdo and her black dress showed off her smooth, tan shoulders, and all he could think about as she talked about her bad dating luck was what it would be like to slip her dress all the way off. He slipped her his card, something he'd *never* done before.

That he and Gillian hadn't had sex in nearly six months was the lame justification he gave himself.

The woman called his cell a week later. He and Gillian were in the kitchen cleaning up when he saw the text and snuck into the bathroom to reply. They slept together once, in the woman's apartment, which had cats and too many plants, and only the once. But then she kept calling his cell and leaving messages. When he didn't call her back, she must have Googled him because she sent him a pile of cat shit in a brown Amazon box. He deserved it. But Gillian was the one who opened the box and of course, she wanted to know who would do something like that. He thought telling her would set things right, instead it blew up their marriage.

Farther up the path, Riley screams. Stephen runs past Eric and Juan to see what the problem is. Mike's hand is on her shoulder, laughing.

"What happened?" Stephen says.

Riley points to an enormous red and black spider spinning on its thread in the middle of the path. She's thrown her phone in surprise and now their guide is parting bushes to retrieve it. Eric and Mike wait with Riley while Stephen helps Juan.

"Got it," Stephen says, triumphantly waving the phone but no one's paying attention, least of all Riley. Eric's telling her about the spiders he finds on night walks, big as dinner plates. Juan tells them about the tarantula he filmed dragging an opossum off to eat. "No more than twenty miles from where we are right now," he says, grinning like it's the funniest thing in the world.

"Despite the warning colors, this spider's harmless," Eric says.

Riley visibly shivers. "They're just not my thing."

"I wouldn't think you were afraid of anything," Mike says. The overt familiarity in his teasing, like he and Riley are best buddies all of a sudden, is waving all sorts of red flags. He's flirting is what it is.

Stephen walks up behind her and hugs her. "Hey," she says, grabbing at his forearms. "Too tight." He loosens his grip but doesn't let go.

Juan and Eric call them over to a tree. Stephen pulls Riley closer for a kiss, but she breaks away. "You smell, baby," she says, shaking her head.

Eric scrapes the bark with a jackknife. "This stuff is great for keeping mosquitos away," he says. "Tastes like ass, but it works."

Mosquitos have claimed the airspace around Stephen's head and neck since the beginning of their trek, but he's not about to swallow another nasty tasting plant. The guide taps the tree's trunk, and a slew of ants scurry out through a hole and make a line for the ground.

"Fire ants," Eric says. "They can mess a person *up*."

"Bugs are so creepy," Riley says.

"You guys ever seen a bullet ant?" Mike asks Eric and Juan. Riley films him as he explains how the Mawé use bullet ants to prove their manhood. "Just one bite from the little fuckers can bring a man to his knees. Worst pain ever recorded. And these Mawé dudes stick their hands into a glove full of them." Mike looks to Stephen. "How about it, Steve? You and me? Face off with a bullet ant? The ultimate test of manhood." Mike gives Stephen's shoulder a playful shove. "Just messing with you, old man."

"More like a test of stupidity," Stephen says.

"Says the bougie white man with zero knowledge of local culture," Mike says.

"Fine then, bring it on," Stephen says, sarcastically.

"Did you get all that, Riley?" Mike mugs for Riley's recording. "Juan, you gonna help us find one of those badass ants?"

Stephen regrets playing along. He should've ignored him. The humidity of the jungle, the mosquitos circling him, the constant vigilance for ugly biting and stinging things has been test enough for him.

The group moves on, Riley and Mike in the lead again, talking and laughing. Stephen can't wait to get back to the center. His left knee is bothering him again and much of his exposed skin itches like hell.

"What was *that?"* Riley lies naked on their bed, dabbing a concoction Eric gave them on her mosquito bites. She's already dotted the stuff on her ankles, wrists, neck, and face as well as a couple of bites near her belly button. Stephen's own face is a mess. He can feel it. He hopes they don't get malaria or some other disease.

"What was what?"

"That nonsense on the hike. You acted like a moron. Jealous and possessive and that is *so* not cool. It's not the vibe I like in you."

He doesn't respond. He's lying next to her, resting his throbbing knee, trying not to scratch the mounds of poison all over his face and neck, trying to muster the will to drag his smelly body into the shower. "He's a bit much, don't you think?" he says, after a while.

"Who?"

"Mike."

"I think he's nice. And it's better to be in the jungle with someone who actually knows things."

"I know things."

"Things that matter *here*." She screws the top back on the jar of bug ointment and sets it on the nightstand near her phone. "I'm going to interview him for my channel. A whole separate video. He knows a lot about plants and the history of this place."

"I thought your reason for coming here was to vlog about the center?"

"I can do both. My viewers want it all."

"You're so thoughtful," Stephen says, sarcastically, but she doesn't notice because she leans over and kisses the top of his head. "Be quiet now, baby. I'm going to meditate."

He's irritated and worn out and that's probably why he's feeling like he doesn't like Riley very much in this moment. "I'm taking a shower," he says, pushing himself off the bed.

Riley's already at dinner, chatting it up with Mike when Stephen walks into the dining hall. After his shower, Stephen air-dried on the bed while Riley got ready. He must have dozed off. When he woke, she was gone.

She's wearing her silky green dress. One of his favorites.

The two stop talking when he sits down. "Hey," Mike says with a nod to Stephen. "We were brainstorming how to promote our manly bullet ant competition on social media." He looks at Riley, "How many hits do you think you'd get?"

"It would totally go viral," she says with a giggle. It's the same laugh she uses for her channel, high-pitched and fake.

The table is laid out with platters of vegetables and fruits. Stephen could really use some meat. Even a fish would do. While he's fantasizing, a glass of cab would be nice, or a small sauterne at the end of the meal. Four days left in this hell hole.

Riley has barely acknowledged him. She's too busy talking with Mike about filming him tomorrow.

"What time are we meeting up?" Stephen asks.

"You'll be fine on your own for a while," she says coolly.

"I thought I was your videographer."

The center's crew, talking and laughing, enter the dining hall with Eric.

"Not tomorrow," Riley says, curtly.

Mike gloats from across the table. Stephen says, "I thought the point was plant medicine. Why would your followers be interested in some random guy?"

"I'm a researcher," Mike says.

"Whatever," Stephen says, not looking at him. Addressing Riley, he lowers his voice to what he hopes is a gentler tone, "Why does everything in your life have to end up on social media?"

"Excuse me?" Riley throws him an incredulous look.

Stephen calmly covers his rice with vegetables. He shrugs. "Why don't you just put your phone down and live? In the moment, like the rest of us?"

"Okay, boomer," Riley says. "I think I'm capable of multitasking. Like, I can record the moment you're being awful while I'm living it. Social media is the whole reason I'm here, and the reason you're here. In case you've forgotten, I'm the one paying for this trip."

He lays his napkin over his lap and shakes his head. "Baby, you think the people who follow you, who tap your page then swipe right, or watch your video for the first five minutes before clicking another one, give a shit about this trip or Peru or ayahuasca? For that matter, do you think they really care about the moisturizer you use or what fashion you wear trekking through the jungle?"

"Of course. *Duh.*" Riley gives Mike a look as if to say, *can you believe this guy?*

"They don't, not really. You act like you're doing the world a service when all you're doing is filling an empty void with more emptiness." He feels bad after he says it. Like he's just told one of his boys his school project sucks.

"You're being mean, right now, Stephen," she says, her voice quivering. "I don't know what's gotten into you, but I don't like this person very much." She waves her hand in his general direction but doesn't look at him.

Eric sits down heavily next to Mike. "What a hike that was," he says, puffing out a sigh. "I'm beat." He places his sun hat on the table next to his plate and wipes his head with his bandana.

"Excuse me," Stephen says, rising from the table. He hasn't eaten anything but he's no longer that hungry. There's fruit back in their cottage. He sets a hand on Riley's shoulder. She stiffens. Outside the dining hall, the evening air is thick with humidity and the chatter of insects and other animals.

Before climbing the wooden steps to the door of their hut, he pulls out his phone. Scrolls through his contacts to find Gillian.

In the Amazon and all I can think about is you, he types.

Is it true though? He has been thinking about her more lately, and he *is* missing her, but maybe he's also missing a woman he doesn't know anymore. Maybe he's given up the right to know her. He deletes the text.

The last ceremony. The shaman's giving the blessing. Stephen is on his mattress, an orange bucket within reach, though he doesn't expect to need it. He hasn't puked yet. An empty mattress lies between him and Riley. They've hardly talked since dinner the night before. She didn't come back to their hut until much later. Stephen couldn't stay awake long enough to wait up for her and as soon as breakfast was served, she was off with Mike and a tour guide on a riverboat. No offer for him to join. He spent the day swimming, getting a massage and taking a nice long nap. Fuck 'em. He watched some of Riley's recent vlogs on his phone and he's not in any of them. In the beginning of their relationship, Riley posted a slew of pictures of him on social media. A couple of times he appeared in a video. On this trip, it's like he doesn't exist.

Mike has claimed the mattress next to Riley. He leans toward her, whispering something. She smiles and blushes.

When it's time for Stephen to take the cup from the shaman, he swallows, the bitter paste scouring his tongue and throat. He signals for another dose. The shaman pours more.

Stephen's fingers feel like they're swelling but they look normal. The feeling persists then spreads up his arms and across his chest. His body expands until he feels his skin could scrape the walls. He closes his eyes, thinking doing so will help. Instead, an explosion of geometric shapes fires off in his vision. The shapes shift and become smaller and curlier. The scribbles come together to form a dagger which takes aim at his heart. The pain rips through him like electricity, starting in the roots of his teeth, moving through his vascular system and nerve cells at once. He's dying. He's sure of it. He's dying and he'll never see Gillian or his boys again.

Then: an image of Gillian at their old kitchen sink. The boys in bed after baths and story time, asleep before he finishes the third book. He walks into the kitchen and there's his wife washing the last of the dinner dishes. She looks over her shoulder and smiles at him. "Down for the night?" she says. He's struck by how beautiful she looks in the warm light above the sink, in her bellbottom jeans and water-splashed tee.

His phone vibrates. He fishes it from his pocket and reads the text from the woman he met at the corporate dinner. This time, in his ayahuasca-induced dream, he doesn't move to the bathroom where he can shut the door. He doesn't agree to meet the woman to "get to know her better." This time, he blocks the number and shuts his phone off.

He walks over to Gillian, kisses her neck, breathes in her scent: a little spicy, a little sweaty, *her*. A smell, he's now certain, exactly like love.

TALK TO ME

"What's he growing over there?" Iris says. "Since when does he *garden?*"

Iris and her husband Dan drink their morning coffee and spy on the guy next door through their kitchen window. It's Saturday morning, not even eight o'clock, and their neighbor is on his knees digging and arranging. Avery's lawn looks like a nursery. Plants and trees and shrubs in black pots squat around him. Empty containers and bags of soil lay scattered nearby. "How on earth did he get it all there and so early?"

"I'll walk over and ask," Dan offers.

"You're going to *ask* him?"

"No use guessing," he adds cheerfully.

He runs water over his mug, his Best Dad Ever mug (Iris does not have a Best Mom mug, has never had one) and leaves it upside down on the dishrack to dry. She'll need to give it a proper wash. After more than thirty years of marriage, she knows dishes left to Dan never see a drop of soap.

The front door bangs shut. Then there he is making his way across their unadorned swath of Bermuda grass, brown-tipped and sunburnt, to Avery, who looks up briefly as he hand-shovels dirt into a terracotta pot as wide as a kiddie pool. Iris sips her coffee and watches.

Avery used to go off to work weekday mornings in his Volvo. But for the last year or so, his Volvo has remained parked during the work week while assorted vehicles come and go behind it, as if he might be dealing drugs or something from his gigantic house. Iris finds the goings-on curious, but she and Dan are friendly with Avery only in that privacy-respecting way neighbors have of acknowledging each other without actually talking.

Avery gets up to greet Dan, brushing dirt from his knees. The two men move from container to container, Avery gesturing and talking, Dan, nodding and following behind. When Avery bends to turn his hose on, Dan gives Iris a wave.

"So?" she says, when Dan returns.

"Herbs and stuff."

"Marijuana?"

Dan rubs a weed between his fingers then holds it to her nose. "Lemon Verbena, or some such. Other things, too, but no, no pot." He tosses the plant on the counter before filling his water bottle for his run. Now that they're both retired, Dan from his insurance company and Iris from teaching art to mostly uninterested high school students, Dan has recently taken up running and resistance training. Her idea of fitness isn't as gung-ho, but she appreciates his wanting to be healthy.

"So what's with his bare feet?" she says, plucking the verbena from the counter. She opens the trash bin with her foot and drops it in.

Dan looks up from tying his sneakers, smirking. "It didn't occur to me to ask about his sartorial choices." He bends and twists his back, then using the bottom rung of a counter stool he stretches his quads. She loves his meaty legs, especially his calves, could bite into them like a pair of Renaissance Fair drumsticks. "You can ask him next weekend when we go over for dinner," Dan says.

"You didn't!" They decided they wouldn't socialize with neighbors when they first moved to the suburbs from their thin-walled apartment in Raleigh. They'd heard too many arguments and rounds of make-up sex.

"One dinner," he assures her.

The screen door clangs shut behind him, and Iris watches her husband jog up the road toward the center of town, handsome with his barely graying hair, his peculiar way of leaning forward as if fighting a wind though the air is still and humid.

She considers viable excuses. The idea of sitting through a dinner talking about plants leaves her heavy-limbed with dread. She resents time-wasting activities like parties and dinners. So few people are actually interesting.

In bed that evening, Dan's fingers on her areola feel like insects asking for a swat. She clears her throat in disapproval. His fingers continue their path around her nipple, barely touching her skin.

"What are you doing?" she says, irritably. "That tickles."

"Good tickle?"

"No. Definitely not."

"I'm trying something."

She shifts away from his hand and gives him one of her annoyed teacher looks. She's wounded him, his expression says as much.

"A kind of mindfulness," Dan says. "Avery says orgasms from present, intentional lovemaking—"

"You were talking to the neighbor about *sex*?" Iris sits up.

"Of course not." Dan looks over at her from his pillow. "I saw it on his blog. He mentioned his Internet following and I checked it out. Apparently, he's a shaman."

"A *shaman*?"

"Pretty interesting stuff."

"*Puhlease.* He's as much of a shaman as I am. Shamans are Peruvian or from Nepal. They're not American pseudo-hippies living in the burbs."

"I don't know," Dan says. "Aren't you being a bit reductive?"

Iris blows out a sigh. "In any case, we're not getting sex advice from Mr. Green Thumb over there." She needs to pee.

Keeping the bathroom light off, she peers through the curtains at Avery's house, which is also dark, save for a light on the second floor. When Avery's naked torso appears in the lighted window, a towel wrapped around his bottom half, she snaps back from her own window as if burned.

The following weekend, Avery greets them wearing jeans, bare feet, and a white tunic unbuttoned at the top to reveal wiry black hairs sprouting from below his collar bone. He's a tall man, as tall as Iris, large, and big-boned but also soft and fleshy in his face and neck. His shirt clings to his chest displaying untoned pecs. Back when Avery had a job somewhere, he looked young and sharp in his tailored clothes and trimmed hair. Now that she's seeing him up close, she guesses he's nearer their age, late forties at the very least.

Iris hugs her bowl of cling-wrapped antipasto as Avery leads them on a tour of the bottom floor. Like many of the houses in the neighborhood, this one appears larger from the outside due to high ceilings and wasted space. She signed up for all the walk-throughs she could during the construction of them and attended the open houses, nibbling on chocolate chip cookies and pretending to seriously consider the down payment and mortgage equations. She loves her own house, an understated, updated ranch, and whenever she's inside one of these newer, pretentious builds, she loves it even more.

Avery's bottom floor is expansive, the walls a bland ecru. In the living area, among furniture too trendy to be comfortable, there's a meandering layer of debris: plastic nursery pots and liners scattered on the floor, plant cuttings crowding the side tables, seeds drying on sheets of newspaper on the floorboards, vials, jam jars, and boxes covering the marble surface of a coffee table. "Business has really taken off. It's out of control," he says, with what looks to be an insincere shake of his head.

If he's embarrassed by the mess, it doesn't show.

"The short-term plan is to build a couple of greenhouses in the back, serious structures," he says. Iris grimly imagines having to look out on this industrious farming any time she wants to use her deck. "But eventually, I'll need to move the whole operation to a much larger plot in the country. Not sure how long this arrangement will be tolerable," he says, gesturing to the spilled dirt and broken plants on the floor. They follow him to the kitchen where Avery finally notices Iris's bowl and reaches for it. "I should've taken this from you already. Forgive my manners."

"It's antipasto." Iris is proud of her salad with its special dressing from Italy she found at Aldi's.

"Ah," Avery says, revealing his disappointment with an exaggerated sad face. "I hope you don't mind taking it back with you. We're strict vegetarians."

"No, no," Iris says, her face heating up. Flustered, she offers an empty compliment of the kitchen which is high-ceilinged and white and nothing special.

Avery opens his gigantic stainless-steel fridge and shoves the salad inside. "It does the job," he says, off-handedly.

Dan hands the weedy bouquet of flowers he'd brought from Whole Foods to a woman who enters just then. Avery introduces her as his girlfriend, Montse. The woman is petite, young, maybe in her early thirties, with a round, rosy face framed by a fluff of blonde hair on top of a long stalk of a neck. She stands expectantly, her pale brows raised, her sunflower face smiling at Avery. He snaps his fingers like he's just figured out what she wants and produces a fluted vase from one of the cupboards.

"Mousey?" Iris says, sensing she heard wrong.

"Montse," pronounces the woman pleasantly, arranging the weeds in a vase. "Like *won't say*, but with an M."

Avery ruffles his girlfriend's hair which sticks up from his fingering. "Sparkling or still?" he asks. "Or we have wine, if you prefer."

Iris asks if there's a white.

"Good idea. I'll have wine, too," Montse says, before making a face at Avery's obvious disapproval.

The dining room is another high-ceilinged space—Iris can't help but gloat thinking about the heating bill in an impractical house like this—with a large painting of an egg on a stool defacing an entire wall. The table is long and farm-style with overlarge chairs. Four place settings decorate one end of the table, potted plants leak dirt onto newspapers at the other. A ceiling fan stirs up the smell of soil and damp newsprint.

Vegetarian turns out to be portobello burgers, cauliflower "tater tots" and a salad. The tater tots are orange, having been sprinkled with turmeric. Avery seems particularly proud of this culinary cleverness. A couple of Dan's jokes fall flat, but the conversation quickly picks up steam when the subject of religion is raised. Dan asks Avery about being a shaman.

"Ah, but shamanism isn't a religion," Avery says, swirling his glass of sparkling water as if it were wine. "Of the spirit, yes, but I have to say, religion on the whole is quite a disaster, don't you think?" A substantial crumb of cauliflower has nested in Avery's beard. With great effort, Iris wrests her eyes away from it as he speaks.

"Iris and I aren't religious either," Dan says. "I was raised Catholic but all those hypocritical rituals turned me off pretty early on. I was lucky. My parents were the kind of church-goers who only showed up for Easter and Christmas."

"Mine were Baptist," Montse says. "Holy Roller kind. Snakes, tongues, the whole circus." She rolls her eyes and smiles, the dimples in her wide cheeks deepening.

"When our daughter Daphne was a teenager, she begged Iris and me to take her to church," Dan says. "She got it in her mind she wanted an invitation to Cotillion and only church-goers were invited."

"She did no such thing," Iris says, laughing to hide her discomfort. Talking about Daphne sometimes feels like treading through a minefield. All of Iris's mistakes as a mother waiting to explode in her face.

"Oh, but she did."

"I would've recalled."

Iris doesn't understand where his assertion has come from. She and her daughter may not have had a perfect relationship but Iris still knew her best. "Daphne hated the idea of religion as much as we did," Iris insists. "What was that thing she used to say? Religion is a meaningless morality code?"

"That was later," Dan says. "When she was studying Nietzsche. Remember?"

Iris does not remember, but when Daphne was living at home, they hardly spoke to one another. Daphne was always a daddy's girl, but the estrangement between her and Iris took root after the incident in high school with the Driver's Ed teacher. After Iris had failed her so thoroughly, Daphne started relying on Dan more for personal advice. Iris was simply a necessary means of survival: food, money, tampons. Later, when Daphne was almost finished with university, she warmed a little, but still withheld the easy affection she reserved for her father.

"She sounds like a smart young woman," Montse says softly. She offers Iris a smile.

"I was partial to Wittgenstein, myself," Avery says, before delivering a forkful of tots to his mouth.

Iris catches the withering look Montse shoots him.

"Yes, she's always been clever," Iris says.

"What does she do?" Avery asks.

"She's an artist," Dan says. "Takes after her mother. Iris used to be an artist, you know."

"I'm *still* an artist," Iris says. She glares at the side of her husband's head.

"I'm sorry," Dan says. "I only meant that you used to show your work in galleries." Under the table, he gives her knee a soft squeeze. Iris moves her leg away. He continues, "Daphne lives in California. Her work has been getting some acclaim. All I know is she does gigantic collages, weather-proofed so they can hang on sides of buildings."

Iris is both furious and wounded that Dan would offer up news of their daughter to total strangers yet forget to tell her. She had no idea her daughter's work was such a success. She's not surprised. Drawing and painting came easily to Daphne. Her early drawings looked effortless. Not only technically, but the way in which the subjects were rendered without self-consciousness. Frantic dark slashes, burning bursts of energy on the paper.

"It must be lovely to visit her," Montse says. "Whereabouts does she live?"

"In the bay area," Dan says. "We haven't been out there yet."

Iris simmers with humiliation. It's no coincidence Daphne moved all the way to the other side of the continent. She knows Iris is terrified of flying. Her two greatest fears, airplanes and hospitals, both involving *giving up control*, have thus far been insurmountable. Surgery has been avoided—though the pain in her hips tells her not for much longer—and her attempt at air travel was unsuccessful. She and Dan booked a trip to see Daphne after she first moved out there. Her body trembling, Iris made it all the way through the line of security, past the grouchy, barking TSA agents, spent an hour and a half pretending to read a novel at the gate while she attempted to meditate her terror into something bearable. She made it all the way down the jetway, Dan right behind her, to place her hand on the cool, imposing shell of the plane, but could not bring herself to step inside.

"So you're a shaman," Iris says to change the subject. She needs a target for her irritation and her host will do nicely. "I don't suppose you use that dreadful plant, ayahuasca?" She remembers watching a documentary about it; the film's producers suggested its use could end mental illness, but the story took a dark turn with a death and a coverup.

Avery shakes his head. "It's much too strong for casual use." He reaches for the salt.

"Apparently, a few people have died from it," Iris says. The food is bland and the conversation vexing. She stuffs tots in her mouth to move things along if nothing else.

"Well, it's safe if administered by a responsible healer," he says, his expression serious. "I've taken it myself."

"What was it like?" Dan asks.

"Amazing. Life-changing, really. But it can make one feel very ill."

"Sounds intriguing," Iris says, insincerely. Montse holds up the bottle of wine and Iris nods. Might as well enjoy a bit of a buzz.

Iris isn't listening to Avery as he explains the work he does. She's still thinking about Daphne. She just wishes her daughter would *talk* to her. Iris has left messages, has even written letters on carefully chosen paper, but all have gone unanswered.

Laughter brings her out of her thoughts and back into the room.

"What was that?" Iris says, suddenly aware they were talking about *her*.

"I was saying what a formidable teacher you were," Dan says. "*I* don't dare cross you, and I married you."

"My students loved me," Iris says, a bit too loudly. Avery and Montse look down at their plates. "They did," she says again, though no one is arguing.

After dinner, Iris helps Montse clean up while the guys check out Avery's mushroom logs out back.

"You must be proud of your daughter," Montse says. "I don't have any children and I probably never will." She bends to rearrange plates and bowls in the dishwasher to make room for more.

Iris rinses the dishes before passing them to Montse. "She's very accomplished." It hurts to talk about Daphne so she changes the subject. "Are you and Avery serious?"

Montse shrugs. "Well, I'd like to be, but he's reticent. He says he's not keen on commitment and what it entails. Like I'm not supposed to ask him to help solve my problems because it's what he does for a living, being a shaman, and his last girlfriend accused him of reading her mind even though he said reading her mind was the last thing he wanted to do."

"I imagine it would be strange dating someone like Avery."

"In the end, he's still a man who farts in bed and leaves toothpaste globs in the drain," Montse says.

Iris remembers the tips Dan gleaned from Avery's blog: be present, enjoy simple touching, practice breathing together. Advice you can get from any dime store guru. Iris is about to ask if Montse finds the sex particularly enlightening, but the men trudge in through the back door.

Crossing their neighbor's yard back to their house, Dan reaches for Iris's hand but she hides it away in her sweater pocket. She quickens her pace and arrives at the door before him, slipping off her shoes once inside. Dan appears in the doorway, looking sorry. She tells him she's taking a bath.

"Don't you want to talk first?" he asks.

"Talk?" Iris has almost gotten to the hallway, but she whips around. "About how you trotted out the fact you're on speaking terms with our daughter and I'm not? In front of people we hardly know?" She's furious and wounded and hasn't had time to sort it all out in her head.

"That wasn't my intention." He walks toward her. He has that look he gets when he's trying to placate her—raised brows, soft smile—which only further infuriates her. "Can we sit down and talk about this?" he says, almost pleading. She knows he's frustrated. So is she.

"I don't want to."

"It occurred to me…and this wasn't why I brought it up, that just sort of happened…but Avery might be able to help you with Daphne."

Obviously, Dan has bought the neighbor's guru act, but she's no fool. "I have no intention of asking our neighbor for anything. I, for one, don't believe he's a shaman. And the one man who could've diffused the situation back then, didn't." If only Dan had stepped in, helped Iris and Daphne sort things out and mend the hurt, they might be speaking today.

"Not this old argument again," Dan says with an exaggerated groan. He walks past her into the kitchen. She hears the *thwick* of the fridge door opening, a bottle cap flicked off. He's having his evening beer, like they're not in the middle of a disagreement, like there's nothing wrong at all.

She follows him into the kitchen and turns on the light. If he wants to talk, damn it, they'll talk. "There's a reason it keeps popping up."

Dan sits at the table, looking worn out. "You caused the rift, Iris," he says, gently. "You were so sure you had all the answers, but you weren't there for her when she needed you."

"And you were? Mr. Oblivious?"

"I didn't know! If you had told me what that piece of shit did to Daphne, I could've given him what he deserved."

"Precisely why I didn't say anything. To avoid unnecessary drama." She doesn't add that she had to continue to work with the man. "But that's neither here nor there. I'm talking about the fallout."

"You downplayed it. What she needed was support, Iris!"

He was right. Daphne had deserved more from her. One night, Daphne told her the Driver's Ed teacher kissed her in the middle of a driving lesson. Iris was confused and scared and didn't know what to do. Now, she pulls out the same excuses she told herself at the time, though she knows better. "You have no idea what it's like to be a woman in this world. One kiss? Women deal with far more. I don't know a single woman who hasn't been groped or worse." For Iris, it had been her best friend's father. "At the time, I thought it would be better for her to put the incident behind her. Obviously, I was *wrong!*"

The Driver's Ed teacher had also been a history teacher and beloved football coach in the same high school where Iris taught art. A part of Iris *wanted* to confront him, but instead, she did her best to avoid him. He was gone a couple of years later—probably to another unsuspecting school. Minutes after the kiss, Daphne hit the car in front of her. She was so shaken, she said, and the teacher told her he would take the blame. Iris recognized the offer for what it was: a silent bargain. Iris murmured something about needing to pay attention driving a car—oh, she had said such stupid things—and that maybe Daphne misunderstood, as if there was anything ambiguous about such a violation.

So many times Iris has wished for a do-over.

Now, she says, "I'm going to bed and put an end to this miserable evening."

She undresses in the dark, forgoing washing her face and brushing her teeth, wanting only the comfort of bed. Dan follows her into their bedroom, turning on the light.

"Must you?" she says, blinking.

"Iris." Dan's voice is soft, void of reproach. She can see he's lost the desire to argue.

She knows she shouldn't keep it going but she's still angry. "You want to think you might have been some kind of hero, but let's face it, where were you ever?" Iris asks. She did most of the work of parenting when Daphne was small. Dan was a new hire so most of his energy went into achieving a firmer foothold in the company. Iris taught art all day and with the rest of her waking hours, she handled house-care and child-care and doctor's visits and all the various painful situations that arise between childhood friends. Oh, Dan offered his help at times, but it was easier for her to take care of it all.

She pulls back the covers and slides in. Her hips are throbbing and she feels ugly. "Hit the light, *please*."

Dan, silent, flicks off the switch, walks into the bathroom and shuts the door.

Mr. Darcy jumps on the bed near her feet and lies down in the crevice between her calves. Mr. Darcy is new, plucked from the shelter. Daphne is allergic to cats so they never had one in the house when she was at home, though occasionally Iris would leave food outside for a stray until the stray realized his charm was ineffectual and his station in life would never improve. Dan first named him Marmalade because of his long orange coat, but Iris renamed him Mr. Darcy for the arrogant way he stomps around, his face stern and expectant, waiting for humans to do his bidding.

After a while, Dan emerges from the bathroom in a cloud of steam. He's left the light on along with the fan. Watching him move about the room, shoulders rounded with age, his stubborn paunch resistant to the running, her anger recedes a little. She does love this man so.

"I almost left you when Daphne was small, you know," she says quietly.

He stands at the foot of the bed, his eyes unreadable in the dim light. "Yes. You've told me that a few times."

"It's a wonder I didn't." Iris pulls the covers up to her neck.

He shuts off the bathroom light and on his way to his side of the bed, he says, "It's a wonder I didn't leave you, too, you know. But here we are, stuck with each other."

She extends a hand to him which he takes and squeezes before climbing in next to her.

"Daphne doesn't call me often, but next time she does, I'll make sure it's on speaker," he says, rubbing her shoulder under the covers.

"You should've been doing that all along."

"Yes," he says, after a bit. "You're right." He moves further under the covers and then his hands open her legs.

"I'm not in the mood," she says.

"A little?"

"Not tonight. Just hold me."

Dan moves up to lie next to her. When he's settled, Iris eases her head into the crook of his arm. They don't have the amount of sex they used to, ironically, since they now have more time for it. It's regular enough, though, and when it happens, it's like a band wrapping around them, pulling them closer, reminding them they are good together. But tonight, she's too drained.

"Don't you think he's strange?" she says.

"Who?"

"Our neighbor."

"He's interesting, that's for sure."

"I think he's pretentious. And calling himself a shaman." A puff of disbelief escapes her mouth.

"He does know a lot about plants."

"Shamans are usually Native Americans, or some other kind of indigenous healer. He doesn't have a Native American bone in him." She has no idea if this is true.

"We'll have to ask him about that," Dan says, sleepily.

Iris has no intention of getting to know Avery further. Her mind drifts to that night at the dinner table and Dan telling Avery and Montse she *used* to be an artist. She imagines pulling her paints out along with her cold-pressed paper, her sable brushes, the condition of which, after all this time, could be unusable for all she knows. Still, a silent firework explodes in her chest at the thought of painting again.

Later in the week, Dan drives their Subaru to the dealership for its scheduled maintenance, so Iris has the morning to herself. She spends a few minutes flailing awkwardly on her yoga mat, her laptop next to her, trying to follow along with the YouTuber, a woman more graceful and fit than she, as she moves through a series of exercises.

Iris is not overweight other than a bit of padding around her middle that came with menopause, but she's also not in shape. She despises gyms, certain she'll be judged by the younger, more sculpted bodies in the room. She also isn't one for running, what with her arthritic hips, but even before the bone-grinding pain, she was never a runner, feeling ungainly and short of breath whenever she tried. Yoga, at least, is doable, so every morning she spends twenty or thirty minutes in the poses she can manage, the number of which has decreased since the progression of her arthritis. Complicating matters are her recent bouts of dizziness. She's only in her late-fifties and she's been strong her whole life, her only medications Tums and Advil. Now, she's looking at stiff bones and an uncooperative body, including the mortifying sneeze-pee which persists, no matter how many Kegels she does.

After Downward Dog, she remains on the mat and pulls her laptop closer to Google Avery Sampson. She clicks on Plants are Life: A Shaman's Journey, and her neighbor's face smiles at her from the top of his website. There are testimonials, pictures of various plants, a blog. She clicks on the blog.

Wild lettuce is one of the most abundant plant allies growing freely and free of charge all across the country. Its milk can be used to calm anxiety, relieve mild pain and it can also help with insomnia!

Iris clicks on one of the video links and there's Avery talking about his process for collecting and storing wild lettuce, and creating a tincture, apparently with a whole lot of vodka. In the video, he looks like he's been living in the woods, unkempt and wild-haired. Of course, he's wearing a yogi tunic like the one he had on the other night. Everything about him smacks of fakery. She skims through old blog topics: different plants and their uses, anti-consumerism movement, environmentally responsible behaviors. And then there's how he became a shaman:

Every shaman finds their unique way into the elusive dimension that holds the answer to every one of the world's many problems. For me, as it is for many, illness was my catalyst. Strep throat gifted me with illuminating visions during my fevers. A problem-solver by nature, I did shaman work unofficially for years while putting myself through school and maintaining a nine-to-five job. Last year, I found myself ready to fulfill my calling.

Mr. Darcy abandons his patch in the sun to rub against Iris's knees before flinging his body onto her laptop's keyboard.

"What do you think, Mr. Darcy? Is the neighbor a shaman or a fake?"

Mr. Darcy considers her, his green and yellow eyes blinking as he stretches his chin to encourage more scratching. She lifts him out of her way to read more.

In trauma, pieces of the soul splinter off until they get called back and repaired. There are herbs that help with this repair, but most effective is a healing session with me. Through drumming, I can achieve the kind of deep trance that allows me direct access to the universe's wisdom. I will work with you to retrieve your soul splinters and restore you to a pre-trauma state. Whether in-person or by phone, these sessions are equally effective.

Like everyone, Iris has experienced a couple of hardships: the death of her mother when she was twelve, the transgression by her friend's father, an emotionally cruel boyfriend in college. In many ways, motherhood itself was a trauma. From the alien takeover of her body, the pain of birth, to the irrational fear that took root in her afterward. As soon as she and Dan brought tiny, wailing Daphne home, Iris's brain was filled with images of all the ways harm could come to their daughter if she wasn't vigilant. Her baby could be accidentally dropped, scalded, her cries misinterpreted. She could suffocate by pillow or bedding or teddy bear. How much fear had leached from her mind into her daughter's? And how much trauma had she unwittingly inflicted?

She had been mostly patient, listening to Daphne describe in her quavering voice the monster peering in through her window, the noises of a settling house, the creepy hand story a friend had told her. Iris took temperatures, made chicken soup from whole chickens, read books, sometimes the same stories so often, she'd read *herself* to sleep. But her patience had a timer. Evenings, after a full day of teaching art, when she would've rather been creating it, she often became short and irritable and sometimes had to make a great effort to be kind. Before she had Daphne, she still managed to have time and energy for her own work, often spending whole weekends in her studio. After she became a mother, she let go of the studio space. Why pay rent for a place she never had time to use? In those years, she was always giving, to Dan, to Daphne, to her students. By the end of a day, she had little left. There were occasions she even lashed out physically: a quick slap on her daughter's behind, a flick of a hairbrush on the side of an arm. These moments were few, but did

Daphne remember them? Did their number multiply in her daughter's memory? Had they splintered her daughter's soul?

Sometimes, folks have difficulty facing the past. Guilt often gets in the way of making amends and healing. I want folks to understand that even if they can't fully commit to a change of understanding, the healing happens anyway. That's the beauty of setting intentions.

Iris's face burns from embarrassment, though she knows his blog can't possibly be referring to her own guilt. She closes her computer and hauls her stiff, aching body off her mat using the sofa for leverage. In the kitchen, she picks up her cell to call Daphne. A generic voice instructs her to leave a message at the tone. "I'd like to talk," Iris says. "About your show…and about how you're doing."

And then, on a whim, she orders a bouquet of flowers to be delivered to Daphne's apartment.

A few days later, Iris is pulling into her driveway when she sees Montse outside in tiny shorts watering Avery's container gardens with a long green hose. Montse waves. Iris gets out and reaches in the back for the groceries.

"Hi there," Montse calls out.

Iris waves and heads for her house, but the woman's still talking.

"What's that?" Iris asks, shifting the bag in her arms.

"I said, it's a beautiful day and come and get some mint." Montse has dropped the hose, water spraying out onto the grass, to pick a handful of greenery.

"I thought plants were Avery's thing," Iris says on her way over.

Montse puts a finger to her lips. "He's inside with a client. If you listen closely, you can hear the drumming."

A faint *pom, pom, pum,* sounds from within.

"How are things with your daughter?" Montse asks.

Iris doesn't recall sharing much about her estrangement with her daughter, but then she'd had a bit of wine that evening.

"Fine," she says.

"I noticed you're a bit stiff when you walk."

"Arthritis. I'm scheduled to have surgery soon." She hasn't even registered yet. She's terrified.

"You know, Avery's a big help with all sorts of problems—"

"I'm afraid he can't rebuild cartilage."

Montse winces. "No."

"Well, I have dinner to start." Iris holds up the mint in her free hand. "Thanks again."

"Before you go…" Montse lays a hand on Iris's arm. "I thought I might plant some catnip for your kitty, if you don't mind. Avery gets so mad at him when he digs up the other plants."

"Really? I haven't seen it." Everyone knows cats will do cat things. Why make such a fuss?

Montse nods. "But if he has his own yummies…"

"Well, you're both problem solvers, aren't you," she snips, but then seeing the hurt on Montse's face, she adds, "Thank you."

It's an unusually warm mid-October evening. No smell of fall in the air, just the vinegary bottom of the garbage can when Iris lifts the lid. Most of the neighborhood is decorated for Halloween. Across the way, a blow-up witch sags, her warty nose to the ground. Earlier in the day, Iris got out her watercolors to see if she still had talent or if all the years teaching art had erased her own ability. It didn't go well. Her paintings muddied, her drawings felt forced and uninspired. She crumpled the attempts and shoved them in a bag for the bin outside. She sets the lid on top and peers over at Avery's yard. His container garden is still lush and green despite winter looming.

She might never have spotted him, if it weren't for the noise: Mr. Darcy digging furiously in Avery's wide terracotta pot, soil and greenery flying through the air behind him.

Avery's front door opens before she can get a scolding word out. Mr. Darcy doesn't even lift his head.

"You little fucker!" Avery yells.

At that, Mr. Darcy stops his digging. He sits in the pot, coolly regarding his accuser.

Iris sees the rifle in Avery's hand.

"Hey!" she shouts. She claps her hands, whether to Mr. Darcy or to Avery, she can't be sure.

Avery looks over and says, "He's been tearing up my plants nearly every damn day."

"That's my cat! You can't *shoot* him."

Iris storms over to Avery's yard. What a fake, she thinks. *Mr. I can't eat animals.*

"I wasn't going to actually hit him," he says, lowering the gun. "I wasn't even aiming at him. A shot in the air might've given the little orange asshole a hint, though."

Iris is about to respond but then her vision blurs and darkens at the edges, like it does when she gets up from yoga too quickly. Her legs collapse like noodles.

When she opens her eyes, Avery is asking her questions. If she feels numb, the name of the current president, and can she follow his finger with her eyes. She must have passed out. Grass prickles the backs of her thighs and arms.

"I think you're all right." Avery says, visibly satisfied with her responses. "You might want to get your blood pressure checked. Can you sit up?"

Mr. Darcy appears near her, purring, rubbing his whiskery face against her cheek.

Iris thinks of Daphne, her calls to her daughter still unanswered. Not even an acknowledgment of the flowers she sent.

She remembers how Daphne's face would become stern with concentration with anything she did, whether stirring cookie batter, or writing, or washing a fork, or making a painting. That same sternness when troubled by something. A friend had snubbed her, she got a bad grade, or maybe she'd seen a homeless person. Iris would kiss the top of her head, breathing in her Daphne-smell, and say, "Talk to me." And she had, until one day she stopped because Iris had failed her.

Avery's face hovers above hers, his wiry beard, his large, dark eyes, his wooly eyebrows. It's a kind face. She sees his concern is genuine. "Talk to me," she says, her voice cracking. She closes her eyes. Imagines her daughter standing next to her father at Iris's funeral, dry-eyed, maybe even relieved. But no, this is only a story Iris tells herself: that her daughter doesn't need her, would be better off without her. She says it again, a whisper, *talk to me*, and imagines the words soaring into the air, riding the currents like terns, making their way across the country to reach her daughter.

Iris reaches for Dan's hand as the roar of engines increases. The plane slowly moves backward from the gate. A baby's cry slices through the thrum of conversations. Iris's heart is fluttery from nerves in spite of the Xanax her doctor said would be a game-changer. She feels her heartbeat inside her like moth wings softly battering a light, but her heart is healthy and strong. Her fainting back in the fall was only due to an inner ear malfunction, so she scheduled the first of her hip surgeries for summer, early June, and the other toward the end of September. Right after she scheduled them, she texted Daphne: *flying to CA to see you in April. Send possible dates ASAP, otherwise, we'll simply show up.* Iris added a laughing emoji so as not to seem overbearing. A week went by before Daphne texted back, her words punctuated with a heart emoji: *the third week would be best.*

The plane turns, still moving backward, then shifts direction, forward, toward the runway. It rolls along slowly, steadily, then stops, the engines quieter, and Iris focuses on her breath, slow and deep. The pilot announces position for takeoff. After a few still moments, the plane thrusts forward, gaining speed, the wheels bumping over the runway, and Iris breathes, in, out, in, out.

Avery told her in their last session that traveling a considerable distance is like a little death. One must think about getting affairs in order before leaving behind work, family, friends, life as we know it, for the unknown. It's a shedding, he said. And then we return renewed, shifted. Iris doesn't like to think about death, lurking as it always is in the periphery, but the analogy Avery used makes sense. At least if Iris dies on this flight, Daphne will know she is loved. Iris may never be a successful artist or achieve any sort of fame, but her greatest contribution will be of her making, hers and Dan's.

Dan smiles at her and squeezes her hand. Oh, how she loves this man, freshly shaved and dressed for the occasion in his suit jacket and jeans. The plane lifts, and then lifts even higher, and Iris cannot bring herself to look out the window at the receding earth. Instead, she closes her eyes and remembers the feel of Daphne's bare skin against her own, still wet and shivery from birth, remembers being able to warm and calm her baby with her own body, remembers the soaring flight her heart took from that moment on. This is what Iris holds in her mind like a mantra as the jet pushes through the air to deliver her to her girl.

NO DANGER HERE

We were exhausted from traveling. I tried to nap but couldn't still my mind. Serenity had immediately closed herself in her room and I worried her doing so meant something. When I knocked, there was no answer. I nudged the door open, expecting to find her listening to music, Air-Pods plugged into her ears, but she lay asleep, her brown hair fanned out on the pillow, cheeks flushed with fatigue or dreams, lips parted. She could almost be my daughter, but she belonged to Richard, not me. My own daughter had had wide-set gray eyes, sun-freckled skin, and a mess of brown curls that used to frustrate me, always twisted into stubborn little nests. I stood in Serenity's doorway and longed to lie next to her on the bed, to listen to her breath move through her body, to take in that sleeping girl smell to which I was no longer privy. Instead, I backed out of the room.

Richard waited for me on our bed.

"Join me," he said.

Ignoring him, I walked over to the window and opened it wide to the smells of Rome: bread dough, diesel, sewage. I undressed in front of the open window, my nipples stiffening in the cool air. Bells resounded from the cathedral near the river. When I turned around, Richard was staring at me, his desire apparent. I lay next to him. He touched my body as if it were his, as if I only existed for his pleasure. His arrogance excited me. I knew this made me a lousy feminist.

"What do you think of her so far?" he asked me, his fingers writing unknown words on my back. The words stopped as he waited for my answer.

"I've haven't known her long. One flight over the ocean."

"Bright girl. The best of me."

"Children usually are."

"Are you jealous?"

"Why would you ask that?"

"I've dealt with it before."

I *was* jealous, but not in the way he probably meant.

"She has a sharp sense of humor," he continued.

I hadn't seen it. To me, she appeared to be entirely humorless.

The first time we met was in the airport the day before. The trip to Italy would be a good way for Serenity and I to get to know each other, he told me when he presented the idea. I was skeptical and told him so. "What if we don't like each other?" I asked. "Traveling brings people together," he said, off-handedly. I'm not sure he fully considered the consequences of forcing me on his teenaged daughter.

Serenity looked like a lot of the young girls did in the movies or on Instagram: thin, dark-eyed, long brown hair dyed blonde at the tips, her mouth held in a perpetual sneer of disdain. She smiled without her eyes and when Richard introduced us, she barely took me in, irrelevant as I was.

We stood near our gate. Our flight wouldn't board for twenty minutes.

"Daddy, did you bring the Xanax?" Her voice was rough, like she had a cold.

Richard dug through his briefcase and tapped a pill from a bottle into her palm. He looked at me. "You want one?"

There was a time I would've had my own bottle of those little white miracles. It's what made the days bearable after I lost my family. But I didn't need them anymore. I told him I was going for coffee. When I returned, Serenity backed into me and coffee leapt from my cup onto her jeans.

"Oh my god!" Serenity stared at the stain as if doing so would make it disappear.

I apologized and handed her my napkin. "I didn't burn you, did I?"

She lifted her eyes to me. Disgust, thick as butter.

"It's not a big deal," she said, though of course it was.

I watched her toe off her knee-high boots and step out of her jeans. Underneath: silky black boxers. People around us snuck glances.

"What? I'm not wearing wet jeans for eight hours on a plane," she snapped at her father.

"Get something from your suitcase."

"This is the empty one. So I can shop, remember?"

Serenity slipped her boots on, adjusted her black sweater so it nearly covered her boxers, and wheeled her empty suitcase toward the crowd now gathered to board.

"Fucking shorts are so high you can almost see her butt," he muttered to me.

I shrugged. "It's what they all wear."

"You being an expert and all." He gestured for me to precede him toward Serenity.

Don't think him an asshole. I hadn't told him about my losses.

Richard had been my neurologist. A couple of years ago, long past losing my husband and daughter, I had these episodes as I was falling asleep in which I was fully awake and cognizant yet unable to move. Sometimes I heard a susurrus in the air above my head; could have been my own pulse but it sounded like ghosts having conversations. He explained the mechanics of sleep paralysis without patronizing. The episodes went away as he said they would and the next time I saw him was at a fundraiser. Three of my paintings were being auctioned off for a non-profit started by a friend. Richard took the seat next to me and under his breath, delivered inappropriate comments that should have made me blush, but instead, made me laugh. That was one of the things that excited me about him: his ability to say whatever he thought without self-consciousness or embarrassment, his ability to reach out and grab what he wanted with only his words.

Later that evening, after the three of us strolled the streets around the Trasteverre, we were back in the flat. Serenity watched Italian TV in the living room, and Richard and I were in our room, freshly warm from the shower. I stood in front of an ornate mirror smoothing lotion over my body. Richard came up behind me and circled my clit with his fingers before slipping them inside. Sex with him was nearly always wordless and I discovered I liked it that way. It was like stepping in and out of another dimension. We talked before, after, but not during. Sometimes he whispered commands—do this, do that—but that wasn't conversation. Sometimes I noticed him circling me like a predator does with prey. My husband had been so polite. Now, polite only got me so far. Richard pushed me onto the bed, face down. He was rough and quick before starting on me with his hands again. Polite didn't feel transcending. Polite reminded me of all I'd lost.

Our sightseeing ambitions began with bones. A set of cement steps led to the door of the Capuchin Crypt. No tickets required. A wooden box near the entry held donations of pastel euros and metal coins. Richard and Serenity read the museum board while I made my way through the crypt, barely breathing. Four rooms; in each, dun-colored bones decorated every surface, bones formed flowers around chandeliers and lacy designs on walls and ceilings. In one room, whole skeletons lay on stone beds, castoff shells. My husband and daughter were cremated after the crash, cremation a decision my husband and I made back when death seemed, if not impossible, at least far, far away; but that was before the woman ran the stop light. There in those rooms, the bones were remnants of life. It might have been a comfort to have evidence of the people I lost. Proof that I had loved and been loved.

One afternoon, near the end of our stay, Serenity and I took a café table outside. We'd been there a week and had three days left before heading home. Richard was reticent to show affection for me in front of Serenity, or maybe he was simply reticent. But my relationship with Serenity was improving. She'd finally begun to open up to me, talk to me about boys and school and what she wanted to do after college. It was a gorgeous, blue-sky day, warm enough to not need a sweater. From where we sat we could see the Capitol, the word ROMA in red and yellow roses on the front lawn.

When the waiter came, I ordered a bottle of Chianti and two glasses. Serenity lifted her brows.

"It's legal here," I said.

"I'm not arguing."

After the wine appeared, her face relaxed, brightened, as she poured a glass for me then herself. That afternoon I learned more about her friends, what music she liked, heard about the boy who told her she wasn't much to look at and then a couple of weeks later grabbed her ass at a party. Her hair was swept back into a ponytail and some of the pieces around her face had come loose. I wanted to touch her hair, tuck the stray pieces behind her ear. If she were mine, I wouldn't hesitate.

The waiter delivered our meals, pasta Bolognese and caprese salads, and when he left, Serenity said, "My father really loved my mother. She broke his heart."

"He doesn't share things like that with me," I said. "We don't have that kind of a relationship."

She smirked, but in a good-natured way. "My mother fell for a younger guy who ended up dumping her."

"It's not my business."

She shrugged, took a sip of wine. "Just trying to tell you why he can be sort of a dick."

"I don't have any problems with him," I said. What I didn't say: I didn't mind that he was sort of a dick. It was what I wanted at the time.

Our last full day, we took a train to Florence. It should have inspired me, wandering through museum after museum, seeing all that art, but my desire to create more of it remained underground. I hadn't painted much since the accident. For me, painting required an ease I rarely felt.

It was late when we boarded the train back to Rome. Serenity and I grew ever closer and Richard didn't seem to like it; perhaps didn't like that his neat compartments were so easily bleeding into one another. He fought for my attention, texting me things like:

I want to make you wet.

His sexting usually had an effect on me, usually heated my body into some kind of life. On the train though, it was a distraction from what really excited me: Serenity. Her chatter about wanting to study law and where she dreamed of going to school, her opinions about the sculptures and the art she'd seen, her movie recommendations. I drank her in, parched.

The train lurched to a stop.

Two men in uniform ran through our car, Italian words crackling on radios.

Serenity looked to her father, then me. "What's going on?" Her voice was high with stress.

A conductor entered our car and ordered us to leave the train immediately. In Italian, French, and English: "Leave your bags, leave everything and depart the train."

We disembarked and made our way with the crowd to a large field. The silhouettes of industrial buildings in the distance stood tall and dark against the purpling sky. People talked rapidly in languages I didn't understand.

Serenity shivered, her teeth clicking together.

A couple from Canada shared what they knew: a Tunisian man claimed to have a bomb on the train, but neither the police nor the dogs found anything. The police took him away anyway.

I could see Serenity allow relief to fold into her body; then, quiet sobs. Richard was still scanning the situation, trying to figure out what to do next.

I gathered his daughter into my arms. Her hair smelled of rose shampoo. Her heart beat hard and fast in the side of her neck. I rubbed circles on her back and said, "It's going to be all right. Everything's fine. There's no danger." I told her over and over she was safe, rocking my words into her body, though I understood how wrong it was to think any of us is ever safe. Still, it was a necessary lie. A lie a mother might've told.

SELF-PORTRAIT

"Fran didn't ask anything about my art. Not a word." Iris digs through her purse for a stick of spearmint gum. "She's so self-centered. Always has been."

Iris and Dan are driving home from dinner at Bill and Fran's house. Dan and Bill used to work together in insurance before they retired.

"What was left to ask?" Dan teases. "You talked nonstop." He glances over, smirking. When he looks back at the road, he has to slam on the brakes to avoid rear-ending an SUV.

"Oh hush. She's never taken my art seriously. She thinks Daphne is the only artist in the family, forgetting I was an artist before I was a teacher."

"She didn't know you then," Dan reminds her.

They pass the shell of the Taco Bell that recently burned. "Such a shame," Iris says of the charred remains. Then, "Did you see her brows?" When Dan doesn't answer, she says, "She's had them tattooed on. What does a woman her age need with trendy brows?"

"You're the same age," Dan says. "I don't see you letting yourself go."

Iris doesn't respond. She recently read people age rapidly in two periods of their lives: their forties and sixties. She's sixty-seven and she's horrified by the ways in which her body has changed: her once full cheeks are now jowly, her skin, crepey, and her mid-section is now stubbornly *present*, a shelf for her breasts to rest on.

A buzzing parade of motorcycles passes them on the shoulder. "They're going to cause an accident," Iris gripes. "Where are the police in times like this? Too busy harassing middle-aged women." Iris got a ticket last month for going fifty in a thirty-five. She admits to having a speeding problem. She loves Vivaldi's "Four Seasons" at high volume and sometimes forgets she's in a moving vehicle. "Aging is so much easier when your friends accept it as willingly as you. Otherwise, your own decay is more noticeable."

"You look great!"

Dan used to tell her she was beautiful. She's been demoted to looking great.

Another car pulls out in front of their vehicle and for the second time, Dan hits the brakes hard, thrusting Iris forward in her seat. She leans over and punches the horn.

"Iris! Someday you're going to get us shot."

Dan turns off the main street. They're nearly home. Iris loves her well-tended ranch house, small and uncluttered thanks to her committed mitigation of Dan's hoarding. It's not a modern structure like Bill and Fran's, but its simplicity calms her, holding the chaos of the world at bay. Much of it remains the same as when they bought it. They've only done a few minor repairs and updated the kitchen. Their daughter's height recorded by pen, still decorates the bathroom door.

"What did you think of their new kitchen?" Iris says. All of Bill and Fran's cupboards were bleached white to match the counters and appliances. So much white made the room look hostile.

"It's nice," Dan says, turning onto their street. "To be honest, I couldn't take my eyes away from the lights over the counter."

"They look like penises," Iris says. Each light was pink and tubular and sprouted from a pair of smaller, round lights near the base.

"They do!" Dan says. "Do you think when they chose them, they noticed that? Like, did Bill say to Fran, wouldn't it be fun to hang a row of lights that look like dicks and see how long it takes for someone to say something?"

"Ha! I wonder! He loves a good joke."

"We have arrived," Dan says, using his old, tired line as he drives into their garage.

The following day, Iris sits at the kitchen table preparing for her show. Navigating the website her daughter built for her is proving to be impossible. Daphne claimed it would be easy, that the template was user-friendly, but nothing about it feels friendly to Iris. She hates computers. She wouldn't bother with a website, but Daphne insisted an Internet presence was important if she wanted to sell her work.

Iris can't figure out how to paste text below her images and now she's done something to make the text box wonky. Frustrated, she calls Daphne.

"Sweets, tell me again how to title my paintings on the website."

"Hey, Mom." Iris can tell Daphne is happy to hear from her. It's such a good feeling after being estranged those few years. Iris made some mistakes, unforgivable ones, really, but Daphne did forgive her. "Send me what you want to post and I'll take care of it. When I'm home I'll show you how do it again."

"Will Stephen be coming?" Iris likes Stephen, likes the way his good humor tempers Daphne's moods.

Daphne sighs. "We're taking a break. He'll go to his parents for Thanksgiving."

"I'm sorry."

"There's nothing to be sorry about," Daphne snaps. Then, more gently, "It's a good thing for both of us."

"Of course." Iris doesn't press for details. She doesn't want to undo the progress they've made in their relationship.

"Also, I have another show in early December," her daughter says. "I won't be able to stay as long as usual. I'll leave on Black Friday."

Daphne has enjoyed success as an artist far longer than Iris. Her work is shown on both coasts and even at a gallery in Turin, Italy, and sells for thousands. Dan once accused Iris of being jealous and she didn't speak to him for days afterward. At the time, Iris was newly retired from teaching and was just getting back into making her own work. Jealousy wasn't what she felt when she considered Daphne's success. Yes, there was a twinge of pain when she looked back on the years she herself didn't paint, but she'd chosen motherhood and she was happy with her choice.

"That's wonderful!"

"The show's in New York. Maybe you and Dad can come?"

Iris is thrilled to be invited, especially since she missed so many of her shows during their estrangement. The first time she and Dan flew out to California and she saw Daphne's work in a gallery, Iris was so emotional she cried and her mascara smeared and stung her eyes.

"I have news," Iris says. "A gallery owner contacted me through the website." Iris was surprised and thrilled to get the email. The only other email she's received on her site was from a man who asked if she liked to take it up the ass.

"Oh my god! What did he say?"

"He said he likes what I'm doing. That we don't see enough of older bodies in art." He told Iris he found her perspective intriguing. "He wants to meet for lunch. Apparently he's opening a gallery soon and is interested in the nudes."

"Mom, I'm so sorry, but I have to go. The plumber is here."

And before Iris can say goodbye, Daphne has hung up.

Iris stares at the blank word document. She's supposed to write an artist statement, but she has no idea how to define herself as an artist all these years later. When she was just out of college, working at a local florist shop and painting in a barn turned into a co-op, she had her first show. Back then she was enamored with hyperrealism. It was a thrilling evening, hearing the praise, seeing the red dots under the four she sold. A mere three weeks later, there was a positive pregnancy test.

Dan pokes his head into the kitchen. He's been busy puttering around the yard. Leaves stick in his hair, which, in his older years, has begun to thin and stand straight up on his scalp.

"I'm headed to Lowe's," he says.

She nods, distracted.

"Hello?" Dan calls. "I feel like I'm becoming the Invisible Man."

"Sorry. I'm in the middle of something."

"Can you look at me for one second?"

She complies.

"I don't know what's going on, Iris, but I miss you." He sighs. "I understand you have things you need to do for your show. I'm not complaining about that. It's just I miss the way we used to be, you know?"

He's talking about the night before. He tried to initiate sex but she simply couldn't muster the interest. No one warned Iris that her libido would one day dry up like a puddle in the desert. The way Fran talks, she and Bill have sex all the time.

"We'll work on it," she says, hoping it's enough to assuage. She hasn't the slightest idea how to get her mind and body to cooperate with her heart.

His face softens as he leans down to kiss her cheek. "Be back soon." He walks out through the garage.

Iris returns to her statement. Lately, her subjects are older than sixty-five, mostly women. She wants to explore aging through paint. Dan thinks her paintings are sexual. If they are, it's unintentional. Maybe men always see things through the lens of sex. Iris's point, if there must be a point, is to make visible the beauty in women society overlooks. There. That's her statement.

Lunch turns out to be more of an early dinner. Bruce McMann—the man who contacted her through her website—emailed to say he had a meeting he couldn't get out of and hoped she wouldn't mind a later meal, with the new time in parentheses. The place he chose is on the north side of town, its interior dimly lit and smelling of garlic. Having lunch out has never been her thing, even after she retired from teaching, and when she and Dan have dinner out, they prefer the French bistro downtown. Iris blinks at the hostess while her eyes adjust from the sunny late afternoon. She follows the young woman through a warren of rooms to a table with a window view of the highway and the pines that line it.

Iris unfolds her napkin. Straightens her fork. There are only two other parties in the small room: two older women talking quietly, and a mother and daughter. Iris wishes she had taken Daphne to places like this, spent time with just her. Iris was always working. Lunches were spent in the teachers' lounge. Plus, if she was being honest, it never occurred to her to do the kinds of things other mothers do with their daughters: getting manicures, afternoon tea, meals out. The girl at the other table looks to be about thirteen. At first glance, the two appear to be enjoying a special moment, but Iris soon notices the grim set of the girl's mouth, as if both the burger in front of her and her mother are nuisances to endure. Well, there you go.

A tall, bulky man enters the room and heads her way. He sits at her table. "The hostess told me you were back here." He holds out his hand. "Bruce."

Iris allows him to pump her hand, then immediately pulls out a mini sanitizer from her purse.

"You're just like the photo on your website," he says.

"I don't know whether to be pleased or disappointed about that," Iris says, rubbing the sanitizer in between her fingers.

"Very pleased, I should think."

She's not accustomed to receiving compliments from men anymore. Of course, Dan says the sweetest things, but the power of Dan's remarks has diminished over the years by repetition and reality. When she was younger, she was often whistled at by passersby. She may have been awkwardly tall, but her legs were long and well-shaped. People often said she was striking with her Nordic features and large, dark eyes, but her looks haven't drawn attention for years.

A waiter arrives to drop off laminated menus.

Iris quickly scans hers, dismayed at the offerings. Nothing she would cook for herself. Nothing healthy. "Tell me about your gallery, Bruce."

"Shall we order first? I suggest the lasagna. And a nice bold, red."

She cringes inwardly. "You should know I'm not much of a drinker." She used to enjoy wine, but ever since her surgery for hip replacements, she finds the taste piercingly sour. It probably has something to do with the anesthesia, how toxic it was.

"Then it will be harder to take advantage," he says.

"A woman never wants to hear the words *take advantage*, in business or otherwise." Iris scolds.

"Ha! True. My apologies."

His nose, she's just noticing, is lumpy and lopsided, one nostril placed much lower on his face than the other.

The girl at the next table is crying into her hands. Her mother's mouth is pursed. Iris remembers those days with teenaged Daphne. Any little thing could set off a bomb between them.

When the waiter arrives, Bruce tries to order for her but she interrupts. "Do you have anything green?"

"We have green beans today," the waiter offers.

"Surely you have a salad?"

"Side salad?"

"With oil and vinegar on the side."

The waiter turns on his heels for the kitchen.

Bruce unfolds his napkin and fills her in on his ideas for a joint show. "I have in mind the perfect artist to complement your work." Disappointment dampens her mood. She'd imagined this man courting her for a solo show. Daphne had solo shows all the time. Was the work Iris did not worthy of one? "This woman also does nudes, though hers are even more abstract than yours."

Iris wonders how much he knows about art if he doesn't understand her work is more expressionist than abstract.

He carries on about this other artist, her background, her shows in other states. Tells Iris to Google her when she gets home, which she won't do. The waiter shows up with the wine and Bruce approves it.

"She does a lot of self-portraits," Bruce says about the other artist. "Have you done any?"

"I have not."

"You'll need to for this joint show, I should think."

"Why is that?" Iris sips her wine. It's surprisingly good. Maybe she's been drinking the wrong wine all along.

"It's a quirk of mine. I ask it of all my artists." He gives her a sneaky smile. "You can tell a lot about a person by how they perceive themselves."

If she painted a self-portrait, which she has yet to do, it would be tempting to ignore her positive features and skip right to rendering the lengthening of her face, the fat hanging like a curtain from her chin, her jowl lines deepening, giving her the appearance of a ventriloquist's dummy. These changes were gradual, they *must* have been, but it seemed to her one morning she woke up to a completely different face in the mirror. And what she couldn't see in the mirror, the thickening of her torso, the extra fat under her arms, she spotted in photos of herself. She supposes there's no point in painting other older women if she can't embrace her own aging.

"Fine," she relents. "I'll do one." She was used to giving assignments, not accepting them, but this is an opportunity she doesn't want to lose.

"Actually, I'd like the whole show to be centered around the concept of self-portraits. Variations on the theme. What do you say?"

"Let's see if I can manage the one, first."

Over dinner, Bruce tells her he's new to the area. He had a gallery in Chicago, but the cold arrived too early and receded too late. He sold his building, moved south, and found an abandoned church for cheap. "It's a short drive from here," he tells her. There's a bit of sauce on his chin. He's not a bad looking man, even if a little overweight. It's only the kind of padding that comes with age. She supposes he's younger than she is, though.

Iris takes a napkin to her own chin. "You have something there," she says.

Bruce swipes at the sauce and tells her he married too soon after college and it didn't work out. He seems to enjoy talking about himself.

"Enough about me," he says, as if reading her mind. "Tell me about you."

"There's not much to say, really. I finished university, thought I would be an artist, but ended up a mother and teaching art to teenagers. I also married soon after college but it worked out, so good for me." She laughs, feeling awkward. "I had one show, and soon after I was pregnant…"

"But you still painted, surely."

"No. The smell made me nauseous." She pauses, thinking back. "And then I had an infant to care for."

"Your work is so accomplished, so assured, I would've guessed you'd been painting all this time."

To hear such nice things deeply satisfies her in a way she hasn't experienced for years.

"Oh, occasionally, I'd pick up a pencil or my watercolors, but I've only recently started back with oils."

"Well, I'm glad you did. I love what you're doing," he says. He mops up red sauce from his plate with one of the anemic looking rolls that came with his dinner. Iris's own dinner, the strings of carrot and slices of pink tomatoes over pale lettuce leaves could hardly be considered good, but she's too nervous and excited to taste the food anyway.

When eventually the waiter lays the bill on the table between them, Bruce slips a pair of readers on, examines it, then places a credit card on top. Then, "This has my personal contact info," he tells her, handing her his business card. "Feel free to text anytime. I'm looking forward to the work that comes from this meeting."

At home, she finds Dan in the kitchen, loading the dishwasher. He's doing it all wrong as usual. "Let me," Iris says, gently pushing him aside with her hip.

"Did you have some wine?" Dan teases, tapping her lightly on the behind.

"How can you tell? I'm not *drunk*." She moves the cups closer together to make room for more dishes.

"Oh, I don't know. Maybe it's the fact your face is bright red, and only two things make you flushed: wine and sex." Dans pulls her away from the dishwasher and kisses her between the shoulder blades. Oh, there, it is. A spark of *something*. Maybe her desire isn't dead yet. Dan smells of rosemary and eucalyptus body wash. Wonderfully familiar.

"Don't forget hot flashes," Iris says. Dan unzips her dress and she wriggles out of it and flings it on a counter stool. "Anyway, how do you know it wasn't sex?" she teases.

"You're always neat with your clothes unless you're tipsy. Plus, you've always been mine, all mine." His fingers reach for the waistband of her spanks. The spell is broken.

"I'll get them." She swats his hands away. "I've got my horrible granny panties on and they make me sweaty."

Dan sighs.

Iris shuts her eyes and takes a breath. It hurts, his silent rebuke. As if she *wants* to feel this way, shut down and awkward. The last time they had sex was before her hip replacements. They went without sex before her hip replacements, and after, there was the recovery and the fear she would pop her new joints out of place. Their intimacy recovered for a few years but then, against her will, a switch went off and just like that, she stopped thinking about sex at all. Back when she was teaching, she heard a couple of women talking about their lack of libido in the breakroom. "I have to fake it for my husband," one of them said. "I wish *he'd* go into menopause."

"Why don't we lie together and see what happens," she offers. She unfastens her bra and slips out of her panties.

Dan looks surprised. "Here?"

"Well, not *here*. I think we're too old for floors these days."

He takes her hand and they walk to their bedroom. Iris pulls the bed covers back while Dan disappears into the bathroom. Lying there, naked under the cool sheets, she remembers her gynecologist a few years ago declaring Iris to be officially post-menopausal and that sex was no longer something she was obligated to perform. "Your tissue is sore and dry because of the drop in estrogen, and your desire is low because that's just how nature works," the woman said nonchalantly as she typed notes into her laptop, as if she hadn't just pronounced the rest of Iris's sex life dead. Well,

Iris wasn't having it, if she could help it. She'd ordered suppositories online. She would be prepared for when her sex drive returned.

Dan joins her under the sheets, his cold hands reaching for her. His touch is too light, too hesitant. They've forgotten how to be with each other.

"Let's just lie here for a minute," she says.

He settles in closer to her. She drapes her arm over his chest, feeling his heart beat in the soft flesh of his stomach.

"Remember that night we had sex and unbeknownst to us, there was a tornado three quarters of a mile from our house?" Iris asks.

"How could I forget? You were wild that night. Must have been the atmosphere riling you up."

"Mmm. We always went to sleep holding each other then."

"Yes." He fingers her hair. It feels good. They so rarely *touch* each other these days.

"Do you want to go to sleep like this?" Dan asks. She appreciates he isn't insisting on more. "Until my back starts complaining," she answers.

Iris wraps a leg around Dan's. "They sleep in separate beds."

"Who?"

"Fran and Bill."

"Did Fran tell you?"

"No, no. She would never admit something like that. When she was giving the tour of the updates, she called the master *her* room and there was an unmade bed in another room down the hall."

"Could've been their son's."

"He has a family of his own now. In Tennessee. You know that."

A while later, her neck starts to bother her so she slips off Dan's chest and rests it on her pillow. "At least we're sleeping in the same room," she says, but Dan is already snoring.

The following week, Dan's out in the yard talking to a tree guy. One of the hickories is in decline and is listing toward the back corner of the house. From the window over the kitchen sink, Iris watches their neighbor Avery stroll over from his own yard, presumably to join the discussion. She loves trees, but she can't imagine there's much to discuss. Half dead might as well be all the way dead. Iris finishes Windexing the windows then checks her phone. Daphne has texted that the new post is live in Iris's website. But there's also one from Bruce:

You were in my dream last night. He's punctuated the statement with a fire emoji. He didn't seem like an emoji kind of guy with his preppy sports jacket and loafers with no socks.

Hi! This is Iris. She is certain he meant to text someone else and it's best to let him know now.

Dan comes trudging in through the back door, smelling like the outdoors. "It's coming down next week," he announces.

"I'm off to the store," she says. "Call me if you think of something you want."

On the way to Whole Foods, her phone buzzes. At a stop light she reads Bruce's text:

Hi Iris. Looking forward to connecting soon. I want to show you the gallery...

A car behind her beeps. She jumps. She's missed the green light *and* yellow and is so flustered by the horn, she hits the gas and zooms through the red. She checks her rearview mirror in a panic. Wouldn't it be her luck to see a police car right then?

In the store she walks the aisles thinking that it was odd Bruce didn't acknowledge his mistake. Wasn't he embarrassed? She would've been. In the checkout line, she takes her phone out of her bag. He's sent another.

Meet me in Hillsboro. Tomorrow noon at 21 Wisteria. It's off Main Street...

In the shower that evening, Iris thinks about Bruce's first mistaken text, how fluttery she felt inside when she thought, for a second, he might be flirting with her. Of course, he wasn't, but what if he had been? She would never do anything to hurt Dan. Still, how wonderful it would feel to have someone flirt with her! Earlier in the summer she and Dan went to see a romcom at the theater. A beautiful woman falls in love with a handsome man—the usual plot—but their lust for each other was palpable and exciting to watch. The realization that she would never know what it felt like to be lusted after like that made her irritable on the way home. She wouldn't give Dan up for anything, but it would have been nice to feel wanted with the kind of passion she saw on-screen just once in her life.

The parking lot of 21 Wisteria is pot-holed and empty save for a silver Mercedes. The small white building is plain, its paint mostly peeled away to expose grayed wood. Tall weeds grow here and there around it. Bruce climbs out of his car when Iris pulls in. He's wearing the same sports coat, same loafers, but a different shirt. He strolls over and opens her car door for her, his smile eager.

"Iris, lovely as ever," he says, pulling her into a friendly hug. The back of his shirt is damp with sweat, which makes her worry about her underarms and that she might've forgotten to put deodorant on. The sun is punishingly hot.

"Come peek in the window with me," he says, trying to grab her hand, but she snatches it away.

"What is this place?" she says, looking around for signs of other people, but there's no one.

"Just wait," he says. She follows him to one of the building's windows. "Used to be a church," he says.

She peers in. A car passes on the road just then, back-firing, making her jump. Her heart settles and she goes back to gazing in at the stained-glass windows throwing colored rectangles over the wooden floor. The windows are extraordinary.

"Isn't that nice," she says.

"Waiting for your art to fill it," Bruce says. He takes off his sports coat. His forehead shines with sweat.

"What do you mean? I thought my pieces were going in your gallery?"

Bruce raises his sunglasses and winks at her. "This is the place I have in mind. For the joint show and for your pieces on a permanent basis afterward."

"I don't understand," she says. "What about your gallery?"

"This is it. I haven't talked to the owner yet, but I'm sure I can convince him to come down on the price if you're interested in buying…"

It's dawning on her, all that he is expecting, all that she's assumed. "I have no intention of buying a building," she snaps. Suddenly, she's too hot. She digs her fan out of her purse.

"I'm asking you to be a partner, not just an investor," he says. "We can get this up and running in no time."

"So there's no gallery, other than this abandoned, run-down fixer-upper?" She narrows her eyes at him, fanning her face furiously. "What a con you've cooked up."

"I never said I *had* a gallery, Iris. I said I found one."

"Are you asking this of the other artist?"

"I should've been more specific."

"You must think I was born yesterday."

Iris finds her key fob and hurries over to her Prius. "I do think you're talented," Bruce hollers to her back.

She's shaking. She puts her car in reverse without looking to see if anything or anyone is behind her, and drives, tires squealing, out of the parking lot.

That evening, Dan offers to take care of the dinner dishes.

"Are you excited about your show?" he says, standing to clear their plates. They had their meal on the screened-in porch. A storm blew through and cooled the air.

"There isn't going to be a show," Iris says, doing her best to hide her feelings about it.

He turns around to look at her. "What are you talking about?"

"The terms were simply not agreeable so I declined."

She can't bring herself to tell Dan the truth. Nor can she tell him about her last ungracious text to the man, *Duck you!* Followed by a vomit emoji.

In the kitchen, she picks up a sponge and says, "You cooked, I wash."

She scours the plates furiously and thinks about the show that now won't happen. Her self-portraits. Maybe she'll paint them anyway. There will be riotous color in the faces, brilliant, screaming color. A woman not to be taken for a fool, the faces will say. A woman with the face of an artist.

WILLFUL BEASTS

The summer before I turned seventeen, my father pawned me off on Tessa Brown, a horse trainer in a neighboring state so I could *shape up*. I was finished with horses, past that stage of my childhood, but I knew better than to tell him so. My best friend, Trig, ghosted me mid-May, the day after he showed my nude selfies to our friends, pictures that eventually made their way around the school the last weeks before summer break. Pictures that said nothing about me as a person, but people assumed they did. My father, for instance.

Tessa and my father were old friends, but that was the first I'd heard of her. I didn't ask how they knew each other because after he found out about the pictures, our conversations were brief and strained. Whenever he spoke to me, he tended to glance vaguely in my direction as if he couldn't bear to look at me straight on. The only specific thing he said was that she had a reputation for being gentle with horses and tough on kids, but by the end of the summer I was pretty sure he'd made that last part up.

My father drove me there, silent the entire four hours. I wasn't talking either. If he wanted to be that way, it was fine with me. When we pulled in, Tessa came out of the house to meet us and invited my father to stay for dinner. I thought he might, but he hugged her and said he needed to get back.

He had to see a job early in the morning. After he left, Tessa brought me in to meet Marie, her cook and housekeeper, a plump woman with large brown eyes and dark hair streaked with gray. In contrast, Tessa was petite with frizzy brown hair she wore in a bun. She wasn't exactly pretty, but there was something interesting about her face, all angles and hollows. She had a face that would look good in black and white.

My jobs for the summer were to muck stalls, groom the horses, and take care of feeding and watering. In exchange, Tessa gave me dressage lessons which were far and few between. I was mostly there as free labor. Her time was taken up with kids whose parents were paying clients. The farm was nicer than any I'd seen at home: a sprawling, multifloored farmhouse painted white with black shutters, a large barn with an AC and heating system, an indoor ring and rolling green hills. I'd been riding a couple of years by then, mostly in a western saddle.

Tightly wound, Tessa did chores quickly and efficiently and expected me to follow suit. She was blunt and to the point. If I did something the wrong way, she corrected me. *Heels down, shoulders back. Watch your timing. Good way to get kicked, picking up a hoof that way.* In the beginning at least, she treated me like an employee. Nothing more, nothing less. I settled in. In my downtime, I read, swam in the salt-water pool, snapped photos with my phone, and texted my friends, the two I was still talking to. A month in, they both got busy with summer fun and their texts tapered off. Maybe the pictures had something to do with it, maybe not. I didn't care either way—at least that's what I told myself. I'd be starting college at the end of summer. New school, new friends, new life.

That first week at Tessa's, I went on Instagram and saw Trig and my friend Callie at his family's beach house. A few other friends of ours were there, too, but I could tell Callie and Trig were together, which, to be honest, baffled me.

Trig wasn't exactly a catch. I mean, he had been my friend, but he was a complete nerd, bony with overlarge ears and a ridiculous laugh. Still, it hurt to see them looking so happy.

I closed out of Instagram and texted my father.

I hate it here

He didn't text back right away. He owned a flooring company and didn't read his texts on the job. He didn't want his crew to know he needed readers which he kept in the truck. But right before I fell asleep, the muscles in my arms and legs throbbing from all the physical work, my phone buzzed. My father.

You need a woman's take on things

My mother died when I was barely a year old. An aggressive form of breast cancer. I don't have any memories of Helene, only pictures of her, forever beautiful and out of reach.

You're punishing me

It's an opportunity, then he added, *a different perspective*

I texted back he was the one who needed a new perspective. I waited for his response but my phone stayed dark.

When the school told my father about the pictures, he asked me why I would disrespect myself. We were sitting in our driveway, the truck still running. I told him the photos were art. Some were meant to be funny. I'd sent Trig a shot of the inside of my mouth, my tongue coated from eating blue M&Ms, the silver filling in my back molar looking like a black hole. "There were only two of my body and it's not like they were porn." He winced at the word porn. "They're like photos you'd see in museums, abstract. *I* think they're cool."

"Now you have a reputation." I could tell he was working to remain calm by the way he gripped the steering wheel.

"You don't understand," I said, determined not to cry. He was shutting me out for being myself, but I wasn't having it.

One morning, midway through summer, I walked downstairs to the smell of bacon frying. Tessa was the one standing at the stove, not Marie. I'd been there long enough to realize with Tessa there was no bite. Not even a bark. She kept busy with her clients. As long as I did what was expected, she was easy to be around. Nice, even.

"I gave Marie a few days off," she said when she saw me.

"I'm not that hungry," I said, my voice still rough from a lingering summer cold.

"Get the horses fed and see how you feel after." She slid the plate of pancakes in the oven and pointed to juice on the table. "Fresh squeezed. Have some before you head out."

I did what I was told.

The horses nickered when they heard the barn doors open. I'd come to look forward to my time with them. Chores kept my mind occupied, kept me from thinking about Trig. The air in the barn was still and humid. The inside smelled of grain, hay, horse sweat and manure, all smells I liked. I scooped the grain, broke apart the hay bales, and replaced their water. The buckets were slimy with saliva: I would have to scrub them when the horses went out to graze. I cleaned the stalls, picking through the pine shavings with a pitchfork to grab the balls of shit. There were four horses plus Desire, the stallion, the only horse off-limits for riding because he could be mean. I opened his stall to clean it while he ate, figuring he'd be too focused on his food to bother with me. Tessa warned me he was a kicker and had once knocked two teeth from an inexperienced farrier's mouth. She'd called him her brat, patting his rump affectionately.

Back inside the house, I washed my hands while Tessa added scrambled eggs to our breakfast plates. Wireless speakers played country music, a genre I hated because it was what Trig listened to. Tessa told me to take as many pancakes and bacon slices as I wanted, which was none, but I grabbed a pancake anyway. She sometimes scolded me for not eating enough.

Framed photos of Tessa posing with various kids and their horses hung around the dining room. Equestrian magazines were piled precariously on a side table. Fancy dishes and crystal filled a large cabinet, and above the cabinet, a glass case displayed show ribbons.

Tessa sat down at the table.

"You enjoying the pool? I saw you out there yesterday."

I nodded, my mouth full of food.

"I should use it more. All that upkeep and I'm hardly in it." She poured syrup over her pancakes. "Anyway, change of pace today. I'm taking you to the beach."

"Cool," I said, shrugging. I was excited but wasn't about to overdo it. "What about the farm?"

"The horses will be fine for a few hours."

The beach was a thirty-minute ride to the Maine coast. We settled ourselves near the water after lugging everything from the truck: cooler, towels, chairs, and a faded red blanket.

"You should put sunscreen on," she said, passing me the bottle. It made a squelching sound as it spit cool lotion into my hand, lotion that smelled of coconut and pineapple. My father used to take me to the lake. One time I ended up with a second degree burn on the back of my legs. The doctor lectured him about sun protection and my father's face turned sunburn red.

I lay on my stomach, pushing something hard, a rock or a shell, out from under my hip before setting my head down. The waves rushed toward the shore, one after another. Nearby, a family of four argued about how close to the water they should sit, while a group of gulls screamed at each other, fighting for the potato chips one of the kids was scattering to the wind. I glanced over at Tessa who lay on her back, eyes closed. Her bikini was smaller than mine. She had a nice body; slender, muscular, more fit than I was. Only the wrinkles in her skin and sun freckles covering her chest gave her age away.

We stayed until four in the afternoon. I kept reapplying sunscreen, but by the time we left, my skin was tight from salt water and too much sun. On the way to the car, we rinsed off the best we could under showers in the parking lot, our suits dripping water and our feet dusted with sand. Tessa covered the seats of her truck with dry towels and I climbed up, the skin on my back stinging. While she drove, I checked Instagram. There was the picture of Trig with Callie. I zoomed in on Trig's face. If I hated him so much, why did I feel so sad, too? Did they talk about me? Did they make fun of my pictures? I thought about sending him a DM. Instead, I unfollowed them both. The road curved with the river, its water shimmering in the sunlight. I rolled down my window and let the wind stir up my hair. When we arrived at the restaurant, it was already dry.

"They have great steaks here," Tessa said. "Seafood, too. You can get anything you want." She turned the engine off. Her hair, out of its bun, had bushed out from the sea air. She looked like a different person. Younger. "Slip your dress on," she said. "Your suit should be dry by now." She did the same. Hers looked like a super long tee shirt. Black. It looked cool. Mine was a year old, a sundress. Definitely not cool, but the only dress I owned.

The restaurant was dim and smelled of charred meat and fish. The air conditioning was too cold. A waiter arrived with a pitcher of water. Tessa ordered the steak dinner and I asked for the same. She asked if my pee smelled funny after asparagus and she had to explain what she meant because I'd never eaten asparagus. My father cooked the same things over and over: chicken and peas, hamburgers and baked beans, and this weird stew he threw together. When I started cooking, I wasn't any more inventive.

"How do you like the farm?" Tessa asked.

I told her it was fine, that it was really pretty, though probably without the enthusiasm she expected. "I mean, I like the horses and all, but I'm pretty sure my father just wanted me out of sight for the summer."

She gave me a knowing look. "I heard what happened. Your dad said some pictures got around."

"Did he tell you I'm the one who took them? That they were just for fun and I didn't think my *friend* would do that to me?"

"I'm not judging you." I looked up from fingering my napkin and saw that her face was kind. "But these days, with technology and the Internet, things have a way of following you, you know?"

The waiter brought our dinners. I cut into my steak, its juices streaming into the dome of mashed potatoes. Tessa talked about college, how much she loved it, how much she had appreciated knowing my father.

"What was he like?"

"We spent a lot of hours studying in empty classrooms. He was really smart. And a good friend."

I knew he had a degree in history, but he didn't talk much about his days in college other than meeting my mother there.

"I knew your mom, too. They started dating at the end of our freshman year. I was jealous but not because I had a thing for your dad. I just didn't want to lose his friendship. I'm embarrassed to admit I wasn't very nice to her at first." She took a sip of her wine. "But your mom was great and I ended up liking her, too." During dinner, Tessa told stories about my parents and the things they all did together, hiking trips, beach vacations, how my parents would precheck any guy Tessa wanted to date.

Later than night, exhausted but almost happy, I texted my father.

Tessa let me have some of her wine tonight.

A few minutes later he wrote back.

Having a good time?

Not exactly.

???

I mean, it's work not a party. I did learn a couple of things…

I meant about him and my mother but he texted back,

Good. That's what you're there for. Gotta get some sleep. Early day tomorrow.

An overnight storm had cooled the air the next morning. Tessa left a box of cereal on the counter. I read a couple of pages of William Trevor's *Cheating at Canasta* while I ate. When I finished, I washed my dish and spoon and headed out to the barn. Bees dotted the sweet pea shrubs, their heads deep in the blossoms.

The horses fed and stalls cleaned, I took the gelding, Bitter Boots, from his stall and hooked him up to cross ties. I didn't know where Tessa was; there were no students in the dressage ring. I brushed his coat, ran a comb through his tangled mane and picked the muck out of his feet. He stood there, almost asleep from the attention, his head hanging low, eyes closing. Once in a while, he shivered a fly from his back or swept them away with his tail.

Tessa entered the barn, dressed for riding. "There you are. Go in the house and get your riding pants on. I thought we'd go off-property today. There's a trailhead across the road."

The chance to do something different energized me. When I came back out to the barn, Tessa had both Boots and the stallion saddled up. She tightened the girth around Desire and he lifted a leg in protest.

I climbed on Boots and Tessa got on Desire who snorted and danced in place for a minute.

"You'll need to let me lead," Tessa said over her shoulder. "He'll be pissy if Boots gets ahead."

We set off, waiting for a break in traffic so we could cross the road. Tessa told me the trail followed an old railway line that used to run through the state. The head of it was at the other side of a large meadow. I was thrilled to be in a western saddle again. To ride for the fun of it. The day was sunny and warm, the sky a hazy pale blue. It wasn't long before the sound of distant traffic disappeared. We rode for a while, keeping a leisurely pace. Tessa picked it up to a trot and slowed down again when we reached a clearing near a stream. We stopped there, dismounted, and let the horses drink. Afterward, we walked them over to a patch of shade under a cluster of tall oaks.

I wish I'd brought my phone. There were so many shots I wanted to take. The log with mushrooms that looked like pumpkins growing on it. Desire's thick shiny neck as he bent to drink. A rabbit in the bushes, so still I almost missed it.

"You're so much like your dad," she said. She handed me a protein bar and tore hers open with her teeth. "You have a sense of yourself. You're no pushover but you're open to learning things."

Her words made me feel seen. I felt my body relax. I wasn't sure I was all that much like my father, but I didn't know him in the way she did. He went to work every day, cooked dinner, occasionally asked after my homework, which I always told him was fine even if it wasn't. He rarely went out on dates, and when he did, he never brought the woman home. He had strong opinions on things, yes, and I supposed I did too, but he was also stubborn and didn't like to admit when he was wrong. I, on the other hand, was introspective. I would've totally admitted the selfies were wrong if I thought so.

"There was this bad situation," Tessa said. "My freshman year." She looked up at a pair of birds flitting around on the tree branches. "A guy I dated started to scare me after I broke up with him. Followed me a few times. Left me weird notes. Your dad, who, back then, wasn't a big guy, insisted on being my bodyguard. Walked me to classes and my dorm. I'm not sure what your dad would've done if there'd been an actual confrontation, but I felt safer, nonetheless. I really appreciated that."

After a few minutes, she said, "We should head back." She shoved her empty wrapper into her saddle bag. I gathered my reins and mounted my horse.

The pace was quicker back to the barn. We trotted through the woods, following the dirt path, weeds and wildflowers growing on either side. I was thinking about my father. How brave he was protecting his friend. Trig had never been that kind of friend. He was a coward. I thought I might hate him. I was imagining how I would totally ignore him if I ever ran into him again, when about halfway home, Boots got a leg caught in a fallen branch. He did a side-step then tripped. I flew over the top of his head, letting go of the reins, something Tessa told me never to do. My horse took off running.

I stood there stunned for a minute before she yelled for me to climb up behind her on Desire. I held the back of the saddle and we took off. We went a ways and still didn't see him. Tessa slowed to a walk. "He's probably back at the farm," she said. I felt awful. I could tell by her tone she was worried if not outright mad. The road he'd have to cross was only two lanes but it was still a highway.

We found the gelding in the barn in front of his stall, as Tessa predicted, lathered with sweat, but calm. We untacked the horses, walked them out, then brushed them down before putting them up. The whole time, Tessa was quiet. I was waiting for her to chew me out, but like my father, she hardly looked at me. When we finished, I followed her back to the house.

"It'll be a while before dinner," she said curtly. She got to the porch steps and turned to face me. "Monroe, you're about to head off to college. You'll need to use the brains you were given."

"I'm sorry about Boots." I was.

"Yes, you messed up, but he's a shit sometimes. The farm is full of willful beasts." She was joking but then she grew serious. "I'm also talking about setting yourself up to be hurt like you did. Don't demean yourself."

"There's nothing shameful about my body," I said, defiantly.

"I'm not saying you should be ashamed, just wiser." She swatted a horsefly from her shoulder. Then she told me she was having a nap and she'd see me for dinner.

I went for a swim in the pool. I couldn't believe she wasn't sending me home for being so reckless with her horse. She must have really liked my father. Afterward, I hung out in my room trying to read, but I couldn't concentrate. I kept going over what Tessa said. The night I took pictures of my right boob, I'd been thinking about Francesca Woodman, a photographer who took nude self-portraits. Like hers, my photo was moody, made blurry with lighting. I looked at my abstracted flesh in the picture and wondered about my mother's breast cancer, how something bad inside her had snuck up so quickly. Had she felt nothing? Would I have the same thing, lurking, waiting to kill me?

I gave up trying to read and went to do barn chores early.

Boots was extra sweet, as if he knew he'd put me and himself in a bad situation. That was the difference between animals and people. After our friends saw my pictures, Trig basically ghosted me, like our friendship all through high school meant nothing. I scratched Boots behind the ears the way he liked. He nudged me for more when I stopped.

Scrubbing the buckets took a while. After that, I dished out grain and brought all the horses in.

When I walked in the house, the kitchen smelled of sea food and onions.

"Paella," she said, when she saw me. I didn't know what it was, but it smelled good. "I *can* cook, you know. I only hired Marie because if it were left to me, there'd be only cereal most nights. "Set the table, will you?"

I gathered what we needed. By that time, I knew where things were, felt almost at home.

During dinner, she talked about wanting to change a few things up. The feed ratios. Move one of the mares to a different pasture. Rearrange the tack room. The food was spicy; my tongue and throat burned. Tessa poured me a small glass of wine, but I gulped my water instead. There was no talk of calling my father to come get me early.

When we were nearly done, she said, "I want to see some of your pictures, but only if you're comfortable."

I froze. I'd already been burned by my friends. What if she saw my selfies and decided I was exactly what my father thought I was? But also, what if she didn't? What if she thought they were cool? I pulled my phone from my back pocket and opened up my photos.

There was the closeup of my eyeball, reddened by seasonal allergies. The mole on my hip, one weird hair growing from it. A closeup of the top of my head, my part like a road through my forest of hair. And there was one I thought was beautiful: me standing nude in front of our fireplace, my back to the camera, light streaming in, washing out my image so I'm barely recognizable. This was the one inspired by Woodman.

Tessa nodded as she scrolled through. "These are wonderful. Quirky, full of humor. But also, beautiful compositions. Do you use a camera, too?"

"Just my phone."

She stopped at the one with me standing in front of the fireplace. I held my breath. Waited for her to tell me it was wrong to expose so much of myself.

All she said was, "Lovely." She handed my phone back to me.

My father picked me up from Tessa's two weeks before classes started at UNC. He seemed more relaxed than when he dropped me off. Tessa fed us lunch and the two of them talked about their college days. They talked about my mother. How beautiful and smart she was.

On the way home, the radio in the truck was off. There was a rain shower when we started out, but the skies had cleared.

"Did you ever think of getting together with Tessa?"

My father looked over at me, surprised, like the possibility had never occurred to him. "She has her horses and I have my business," he said. Then he added, "Good friendships are rare."

He had a point.

"Tessa's cool," I said.

"You had a good time? Learn a lot?"

I thought for a minute. "I learned mistakes aren't the end of the world."

"Mmm." My father's jaw worked over a problem in his head.

"I'm going to be fine, Dad. Really."

When we pulled into our driveway, hours later, he grabbed my suitcase and we headed for the front door. For the first time in months, he looked at me, really looked at me. He nodded, then turned to walk up the porch steps.

TELL ME WHAT TO DO

Paula hadn't expected a feminist exhibit. Whatever Jonathan is, he's not a feminist. But when she looks again at his text instructing her to watch a certain film in a nearby art museum, she sees he's changed the exhibit's title, with dark humor so typical of him, from "My Body, My Rules," to "Your Body, My Rules." She wanders the museum rooms, only vaguely taking in the art until she finds the film.

The small theater is dark so Paula must feel her way to a seat against the back wall. On-screen, a young woman sits still and stoic on a wooden stool as her shirt, a pale blue button-up, damp in patches, undulates. The woman's face, shiny with sweat, shifts between expressions of pain and ecstasy. The fabric of her shirt bulges with the movement of eels beneath. The display is both fascinating and repulsive.

Jonathan's last text that morning: *Watch the film. Team pain or team pleasure?*

She leaves the theater. Deletes his text without answering.

Graphic imagery and riotous colors cover the walls in a nearby room. A young boy stands next to an older woman—his grandmother, maybe. The surly expression clouding his little face reminds Paula of Dillion, her younger brother, the age he was when she last saw him. Her brother was always scowling like that, trying to make sense of the world. The boy's not looking at the art. He's velcroed his face, red and blotchy like he's been crying, to the woman's hip. The boy looks over at Paula, shapes his hand into the form of a gun and points it at her. Pow, his mouth says silently. He's only a kid acting out, but still, his action feels aggressive.

Later that evening, Paula's in bed, ticking through her work emails on her laptop. Her phone buzzes. A text from Jonathan.

Well? What did you think of the film?

I didn't see it after all. Busy.

Too bad, he texts. *Family's here. Talk with you later.*

She deletes his text without replying.

Paula met Jonathan at a fundraiser for Magnolia House, the domestic violence shelter she runs. He's one of the organization's most generous donors. His mother had an abusive relationship after his father died—this he only told her recently, in a rare moment of meaningful conversation. At the event, Paula first spotted him talking to the board chair. Not conventionally handsome, but then most attractive men weren't. He introduced himself and she recognized the name.

"I want my art to be beautiful or truly provocative and these are neither," he said of the pieces on auction. The event space, a renovated barn, was given to them for the evening, free of charge. Their community's most respected artists, two female professors from a nearby university donated five paintings each. He stood next to her, swirling ice in his empty glass. His voice was soft. She had to lean in to hear him.

"Maybe we're just not clever enough," she said, generously. *She* had no problem understanding them. One artist's work showed variations of the inside of a screaming woman's mouth, and the other featured mountainous piles of laundry in pastel colors.

"You're the executive director," he said. "I've heard good things about you, that you've modernized things, brought in new donors, myself, included." One side of his mouth lifted into a smile. Her eyes were drawn to his lips, full and pale.

"To be honest, Magnolia House wasn't on my radar until I saw your picture in the paper."

His arrogance was attractive, though she wouldn't admit it out loud. She withdrew a business card from her evening bag. His fingers, cool from the ice, lingered on hers as he accepted it. "If there's anything we can do to inspire another generous donation, please let me know," she said.

He lifted his glass, excusing himself. "I'll be in touch."

The first inappropriate text she received from him arrived after an initial discussion on charitable gift options: *tell me what makes you wet.*

Oops, she texted back. *Wrong woman.*

Not the wrong woman.

She was alone in her car, but embarrassment still fired up her face. She pulled over onto the edge of someone's drive and considered her answer. It had been a long time since a man flirted with her so boldly. She was a year away from turning thirty-one. Since her divorce two years prior, she made a point to avoid meeting men, both online and in real life, especially married ones. She didn't want the complication.

She wrote: *That's a question for another time, then.*

Tell me now.

Aren't you married?

I am but here's the deal. We're not going to have sex. We'll just talk about it. No harm. So how about it?

Who was he kidding, thinking there'd be no harm?

We'll see, she texted back.

That was a year ago.

Paula's in Miami for a conference. A three-day event held at the Intercontinental, its theme, the prevalence of child slavery. The speaker—wild-haired, animated, arms covered in crashing gold bangles—paces back and forth in front of the room. "Children come to believe they won't survive without their captors," she says into her microphone.

Paula used to imagine the person who stole her little brother was a woman desperate to have a child. Unmarried, lonely, long past the ability to bear a child herself. Paula imagined the woman driving away with her brother safely buckled into the back seat, to a farm three states away, with goats or llamas, a vegetable garden, a field of sunflowers, and a large, sloped-floored farmhouse. She used to hope the woman would tire of mothering the child she'd stolen and deliver him back. Of course, these were only fantasies. She knew she'd never see her brother again, felt the truth of this deeply, even before the private investigator she hired years later concluded as much. She doesn't dwell on the darker possibilities.

The speaker wraps up with questions from the audience. Paula stands to leave; she's not interested in the Q&A. She's tired. She wants a shower, a bed. She hasn't received a text from Jonathan for days. Maybe he's busy with family. Maybe it's the beginning of the end which she believes will be a good thing. It's not a physical affair, but it *is* inappropriate and lately he's been pressing for more. Other than this one silent week, his texts light up her phone almost daily.

"Nice hair," the man next to her says as he pushes in his chair.

Paula's colored her long blonde hair a lilac gray, a color that usually confuses men on the street, eliciting double-takes. "Thanks," she says, and in case the man thinks his compliment is some kind of opening, she heads for the exit.

Back in her room, she slips into a silk chemise. She likes nice lingerie, likes the feel of silk, the way it drapes over her body. In the months preceding the end of her marriage, she wore ratty T-shirts. They didn't have sex often enough for her husband, and the more he pushed, the more she resisted.

She selects a single-serving bottle of Jack Daniels from the mini fridge to go with the can of Coke she snagged at dinner. Her drink fizzes on the nightstand while she checks her phone.

What are you doing? Jonathan. Sent twelve minutes earlier.

In bed.

She flips through the channels, the sound muted while she waits for his response. Sometimes, if she doesn't answer him right away, he'll go silent for days, days that used to feel cruel, but lately, like a relief.

What are you wearing? he texts.

The bra and panties you told me to buy.

Good. Touch yourself.

She flips through more channels.

Are you wet?

Yes, she lies.

Take off your panties and tell me what you want me to do to you.

She considers copying and pasting from a scenario she sent him last month. She doesn't have the energy to come up with something new. Jonathan's texts have become repetitive, but more annoyingly, have veered away from what she told him she really wants—direction, attention—back to an unimaginative and sexual nature. She could ignore his last text, pretend she never received it. Instead, she changes things up a bit.

A couple got on the elevator today and stood there looking at the changing floor numbers while their little terrier peed on the floor.

Not in the mood?

It's called conversation.

You're tired. Talk tomorrow.

She sets her phone face down on the nightstand and turns the television off.

The following week, Paula stops off at Whole Foods. It's late. After seven. She usually enjoys cooking, it's one of the ways she unwinds, but her day of work meetings has drained her.

Jonathan and his wife Catherine appear before her in the wine section. The sight of him in the grocery store doing normal husband things catches her off guard. It's too late to turn around. He's already seen her. She continues down the aisle, scanning bottles of wine but not taking any of the labels in. As she passes, she gives their cart a quick glance: butcher-papered packages, bananas and melons, plastic baggies of vegetables. She *knows* he's seen her. It would feel less awkward if he'd said hello.

At the checkout line, Paula finds herself standing behind them after the man before her turned around and left, mumbling he had forgotten something. Jonathan's wife is petite, her dark hair pulled off her pale, thin face. Her eyes, large and dark, tilt up awkwardly, like so many women's do after they've had too much Botox.

"I thought that was you," Paula says when Jonathan catches her looking. Catherine's expression, when she glances back, is dismissive. If she knows who Paula is, or cares, she doesn't show it.

Jonathan smiles coolly and makes introductions, but the twitching of the muscles in his jaw gives away his irritation.

"Magnolia House is grateful to both of you," Paula says, though Jonathan's never brought his wife to a single fundraiser. Paula has no idea if she even knows about the checks, how large and frequent they are.

Catherine smiles vaguely and nods, confirming Paula's suspicion, then it's their turn to check out.

Before they leave, Jonathan says, "Good to see you, Miss Helprin. Keep up the great work."

Later that night: *What the fuck was that?*

Paula's on her sofa, binge-watching episodes of Fleabag. *Manners.*

You got in line behind us on purpose.
You're ridiculous.
What are you wearing?
Nothing.
Nice. Take a shower.
Already did.
I want you to get in the shower. Wash yourself again.
Paula feels a spark of the old thrill ignite.
Soap your whole body so it's slippery and wet.
The soap she uses smells of gardenias. She takes her time, smoothing the lather over her breasts, down her arms, between her legs. In the beginning, Jonathan's directions, his *commands,* the specificity of them, were what excited her. He used to tell her what to wear to work, what book to read, what to cook for herself on a given night. She can't explain why her body responds to commands the way it does. Lately, his texts have been only sexual and she finds them less interesting, less able to deliver the calm that arrives with following ordinary instructions. In the shower, it's almost as if he's there with her, *his* hands on her body, his direction guiding her, his attention soothing her. When she turns the shower off, she grabs her phone and snaps a photo of the beads of water clinging to the glass, her bar of soap, glistening on the teak bench, and hits send.

He responds quickly: *Good girl.* His words are like a balm.

When her father moved away, leaving her, her mother, and Paula's younger brothers behind, her mother had to work twelve-hour shifts at the hospital. Paula helped with chores and childcare. Sometimes, Grant snuck out of his room during nap time and Dillion tested her patience with his onslaught of questions impossible to answer. Paula, the responsible one, a *good girl* for years until the afternoon Paula's boyfriend called and she talked to him for over an hour, her fingers twirling her long blonde hair while he told her, his voice low and full of lust, how much he wanted to kiss her and do other things, things that made her face hot and her palms sweaty. Paula was fourteen, Grant, nine, and Dillion, seven. The call ended and the emptiness of the house, its dead silence, lapped at her. She found Grant outside on his hands and knees, ramming a plastic dump truck into a broken toy firetruck. "Where's your brother?" He glanced up from his violence but said nothing. "*Where?*" Paula said, more urgently, and Grant responded, "He went to get ice cream with some lady," as if it were the most natural thing, as if Paula hadn't told them, countless times, not to go off with strangers. The police were called. Their father arrived from California to take Grant for the rest of the summer and hardly looked at Paula while he waited, grim-faced, in the foyer for Grant to finish packing. For weeks afterward, Paula listened to her mother update anyone who phoned. "I pray he's still alive," her mother would say at the end of the call, calls that came less and less frequently. Eventually, people stopped asking about Dillion.

Magnolia House is an old Georgian-style mansion reconfigured into four two-bedroom apartments on the second floor, with central offices, public bathrooms, and seating areas on the first. On Monday, a new woman is brought in and assigned to the fourth apartment. There are procedures to follow whenever someone is offered a spot: a fine-tuned system involving a psychiatrist, social workers, legal counselors, the board of directors, and Paula. At the end of the day, Paula's leaving her office when she runs into the new woman, Michelle, sitting alone on the common room's largest sofa, legs tucked under her, staring at the muted television. The rest of the staff has left for the day.

"Are you okay?" Paula says. "Do you need anything?"

The woman's eyes slowly shift from the television to Paula. Red-haired, pale, so thin her collarbone hangs below her neck like a shelf. Broken blood vessels spider over her face near her eyes and fingerprint bruises circle her neck. Normally, the women stay in their apartments during office hours and only appear in the common areas before appointments.

"I'm Paula. The director here." Paula extends her hand. Michelle slowly meets it with her own. Xanax, Paula thinks. Or something similar.

"I'm trying to decide whether or not to stay," Michelle says slowly, her voice raspy. She looks down at her fingers as they smooth the tassels of the pillow in her lap. She lowers her voice so that Paula must move closer to hear her. "I couldn't have his kid," Michelle says, still looking down. "He's got a bad temper. I can't have a kid with him." Michelle lifts her gaze to Paula. "I still love him, though. Why do I still love him? What's wrong with me?"

Paula sits in the wingback near the sofa. "Attachment like yours is normal. Clarity comes with time."

"He's gonna be *so* pissed," Michelle says. "Are you sure he can't find me?"

Paula's careful to avoid guarantees. "We have security. Very few know about this place and fewer know its location."

The light from the television becomes brighter with a commercial and evidence of stress shows on Michelle's face, her bloodshot eyes, the dark half-circles underneath.

When Paula was in her sophomore year of college, her boyfriend Mark almost killed her. He ran a construction company, a business handed to him after his father's retirement. Mark was handsome, hard-working, funny. She believed she was in love. But when he drank, his jealousy bloomed, toxic and irrational, and he would accuse Paula of having sex with random men on campus—another student, a professor—it didn't matter who. He would rant about the money wasted on school, tell her she didn't need to work, grill her about who she saw each day. She finally broke up with him after having to pry his fingers from around her neck.

"It gets easier," Paula says. She crosses the room to the cascade of ferns on a wooden stand and checks the soil for dryness. "We could use more plants in here, yes?"

Michelle looks around and shrugs, hugs a cushion to her stomach.

"Stay the night. If you feel the same way tomorrow, we'll go from there."

Finally, a nod, a smile.

"See you tomorrow then." Paula sets the alarm on the way out of the house.

A package sits on the ground in front of her apartment. She scoops it up as she lets herself in, her thoughts still on work, on the never-ending fundraising needs. The contents are unlikely to be anything dangerous, but she's apprehensive, nonetheless. After knifing the box open, she pulls out a book of correspondence between Henry Miller and Anaïs Nin, and underneath, wrapped in tissue, is a black, silk slip dress. A note: *The book made me think of us. Wear the dress and meet me Friday evening. I'll text you the address.*

Returning the items to the box, she slips off her shoes and plates the premade salad left over from the night before. She pours herself a glass of Sancerre. The gifts irritate her, feel intrusive. It's not that she doesn't like sex, but for the last few years, she's felt ambivalent about it. No one is more surprised about that than she. For five years she and her ex-husband tried. They got along well enough, there were no dramatic, emotional scenes, but sex was also unemotional, something to be checked off, rote and uninspiring. Feigning desire felt disingenuous. She's grown accustomed to not needing sexual intimacy. A more intimate relationship with Jonathan would change everything.

Later, she refills her glass and calls her mother. After Dillion's abduction, her mother went through periods of not leaving her bed and eventually went from work-leave to picking up extra shifts. She dated strange, disheveled men, often much too old for her. She wasn't unkind to Paula, but she meted out attention in spare, unfocused doses. Her mother still lives in the same house, though Paula doesn't understand why. Even now, her mother's zest for life is flimsy, their exchanges empty.

"Hey," Paula says, when her mother answers.

"I was just thinking about you," her mother says, her voice nasally like she's been crying. "I was thinking about the game you used to play outside with the boys. How you pretended to be shipwrecked and had to live off the land to survive? I used to have to threaten you all to get you to come inside for supper."

Paula remembers those late afternoons and how tired she was doing homework long after her brothers were asleep.

"Will you be coming home for Christmas?" her mother asks. "I think Grant's bringing Ned."

Grant and Ned have been living together for a couple of years. Paula had already met Ned when she flew out to visit, but this will be Grant's first time bringing him home to meet their mother. "I'm not sure yet."

"Would be nice to have the whole family here," and there's a long pause, before her mother says, predictably, her voice softer, "but I guess we'll never have the *whole* family."

After a few more minutes of small talk, Paula says, "I need to go, Mom. Love you lots. I'll let you know about the holiday."

Paula agrees to meet Jonathan Friday evening. The restaurant is on the fifteenth floor of a downtown boutique hotel. She almost asked her Uber driver to turn around, but she didn't, and now she sits across from him, tucked away in a corner of the dimly lit dining room.

She and Jonathan have only been alone together a couple of times in the year she's known him. Once, in the back of a movie theatre, they sat side by side, not touching, watching a steamy foreign film about a voyeur. The last time was more recent, in her office, after the staff had gone home. It was where he told her about his mother, why organizations like Magnolia House were important to him. He was polite that evening, but she could see in the expressions he made, in his awkwardness around her, that he was inwardly struggling, that he wanted more from her.

The waiter delivers their drinks and they talk of potential growth for Magnolia House. After a bit, silence falls between them, which Paula fills with a description of her turbulent flight back from Miami.

When the appetizers come, Paula says, "So, why are we here?"

Jonathan places his fork on his plate and drinks his wine, regarding her. "I decided it was time," he says, loosening his tie. "I'd like to see you, actually *be* with you, not just talk about it."

"Not really our thing, though."

"Maybe I want to change the rules."

"You're married," she says. "You're not available for changed rules."

"What if that were no longer an issue?" Jonathan butters a roll, eyes on her, his one-sided smile lifting a corner of his mouth. He's clearly expecting her to feel excited, grateful even. "I may be taking a break from my marriage," he continues. "I'll be moving into a condo near my office."

"I'm sorry to hear that."

His eyebrows rise as if he's incredulous. "I'm offering you more." He tops his wine off again, though it's still nearly full.

She doesn't respond. When their waiter comes to the table, she asks for more water. They finish the rest of the meal in awkward silence. Neither is interested in dessert.

"We can spend time together tonight," he says, pulling his credit card from his wallet. "I have a room here."

Paula considers what he's suggesting. "Are you *telling* me to come to your room, Jonathan?"

"If that's what you want."

He wears his need on his face. This was his endgame all along and she knows, even as she nods in agreement when he tells her to finish her wine before meeting him in room 612, whatever was between them is over.

It's near the end of September. The dark arrives earlier and holds a hint of the chill to come. Paula hasn't seen or heard from Jonathan since their night at the restaurant. She's not sure how long he waited for her in the hotel room, but surely after an hour or two, he understood she wasn't interested in sleeping with him.

She's on her way out to her car after work, much later than usual, preoccupied with plans for the upcoming gala, when a man approaches her. The parking area is dim; one of two streetlights is out.

"Can I help you?" she says, making sure her irritation is obvious in the tone of her voice, a sigh preceding the question. She's exhausted. It's been a day of meetings, in one of which she had to tell the board she wasn't sure why Jonathan Kilpatrick had seemingly withdrawn his support, worried her face gave away the lie.

Before she can make sense of the situation—a man emerging from a strange car in the staff parking lot—he's already there, a tall man in a sweatshirt and jeans, pointing a gun at her.

"Get in the car," he says. His voice is thin, young sounding.

She's trying to discern, through a flood of thought-stopping adrenaline, which car he means, his or hers, but then he's demanding her keys and phone. With a shaking hand, she fumbles through her bag for the feel of her key fob, but there's so much to sift through—receipts, notes, gum, wallet, tampons, tubes of lipstick—that it takes her longer than he likes.

"Hurry the fuck up," he says, sounding more petulant than dangerous.

Her fingers find the key. She hands it to the man along with her phone. She's still working to figure the best way out of the situation. She's been trained for a moment like this, but she can't shake the shock slowing her thoughts, her actions. He takes the key, shoves her phone into his back pocket, and keeping the gun on her, leads her by the arm to the passenger side. After the lock beeps, he opens her door and nudges her in.

While he's walking around to the driver's side, Paula considers bolting out of the car and running away as fast as she can, but she doesn't see how escape is possible. Fear has made her slow and clumsy, and there's the gun. A bullet will always be faster. The door opens and the man climbs in, turns the engine over, and then he's reversing, turning, and before she's buckled her seatbelt, he's peeling out of the parking lot onto the quiet, empty road.

"Put some music on," the young man says.

"You have my phone."

"Turn on the fucking radio!" He bangs his palm against the steering wheel. "You have a radio in this thing, right?"

With a shaking hand, she chooses the first station she lands on, classic rock, and lowers the volume. The man's left hand clutches the wheel and his right cradles the gun in his lap. They reach the end of the country road and then turn toward the city. Businesses line both sides of the highway, sporadic at first, then closer together as they drive along the strip mall toward the center of the city. At a stop light, Paula gets a better look at him. He's thin. Hair sprouts from his head, untamed and wavy, to his nape. His brows, thick and dark, hang above a prominent nose and stubbled face. The city's bright lights reveal his youth. They pass KFC,

Burger-King, a brightly lit but empty Kwik-Mart, First Bank, and a gun shop.

"Which way to your place?" He looks over at her.

"Why don't you let me drive you there?" With great effort, she makes her voice agreeable.

"Just tell me!"

She sits up straighter; notes the buildings they pass. In her nervous state, it's hard to think of street names, how to direct him, but she manages, turn after turn, until eventually they're sitting in her building's parking area.

The apartment building where she lives is three stories, with two apartments on each floor. The foyer is lit, otherwise all the visible windows are dark.

Her hand reaches for her door handle, but the young man shifts his gun. "Don't move. Don't you fucking move."

She returns her hand to her lap.

The car's engine fan hums. After a time, he says, "What has she said about me?"

"Who?"

"Michelle," he says, his voice cracking. "My girlfriend."

This revelation surprises her. This scrawny young man has sent Michelle to the emergency room three times, once for lacerations inside her uterus, another for a missing eyetooth and head trauma, and this last for strangulation.

"I'm the director. I don't counsel."

"Not everything she says is true."

Paula's mind is sharpening. Remembering specifics about her training calms her. She considers offering him a cost analysis of holding her at gunpoint, of kidnapping her. Men are attracted to logic, respond to it. She talked Mark out of killing her by listing all the ways doing so would hurt *him*.

"You don't know her. She'll have you all fooled, thinking she's all sweet and innocent but she's not."

As he continues his rant, Paula studies him. He's not much younger than Dillion would be. She doubts her brother is still alive, but if he were, what kind of man would he be?

"She went to the clinic," the young man says, his voice softer. "I told her to wait, we'd work things out, but she went ahead and killed the kid, *my* kid."

Paula can't imagine this guy being a father, as violent as he is.

"What did you *think* would happen?" Paula snaps, against her better judgment.

A light goes on in a neighbor's window, illuminating the inside of the car.

"Why didn't she at least talk to me about it? I have rights!" His eyes shine with tears. "I didn't used to hit her. She makes me do it."

"Do you actually believe what you're saying?" Paula knows she should be afraid, that he could take her life in the span of a breath, but all she feels is anger.

Then his body is shaking with sobs. Paula shifts in her seat, pulls the boy toward her, inviting him to lean in. He sinks into her shoulder, tears and snot dampening her blouse. He rocks slightly, still crying. She holds him firmly, quietly. It helps to imagine the boy in her arms is Dillion, that it's Dillion she's comforting.

Paula's right hand reaches for the gun, taking it from him. She doesn't have to pull hard; he releases it willingly. She knows he could take it back, that she hasn't won control of the situation like she's been trained to do. He still has the power.

"What do I do?" the boy sobs into her shoulder. "Tell me what to do."

YOU LOOK SO BEAUTIFUL IN THIS LIGHT

The hologram of Valerie's late husband, Matthew, malfunctioned only a few days after she'd had the service installed. She woke Saturday morning, her eyes gritty like sandpaper and swollen from watching back-to-back tragedies on Netflix. The sunshine trumpeting in through the apartment's floor-to-ceiling windows felt aggressive. She still wasn't used to all the light in Miami. She'd moved here for Matthew, for his new job teaching at the local university. Six months after they moved into the apartment, both employed, already joking about eventually being underwater, he killed himself with too many pills, pills she missed in her search before the move.

There was no note, but she hadn't needed one. She'd known all along his commitment to life, their life together, had been tenuous.

She lowered the shades against the glittering view of Biscayne Bay and positioned the hologram machine. She couldn't pretend to understand how it worked but it was miraculous! When she'd first tried it, there he was, her husband, standing before her looking so real, she forgot herself and went to touch the scruff on his cheek. Her hand slipped through the air without disturbing his image. Today, though, coffee in hand, she pushed a button and Matthew's hologram brightened, faded, then brightened again before disappearing altogether. She tried resetting it the way the instructions advised. Nothing. She called customer service and had a new machine delivered within the week.

The next time it acted up, Valerie was standing in the kitchen venting about work while chopping onions for a Bolognese. Matthew, or rather, an ethereal copy of him, sat on a stool on the other side of the marble counter. With its enhanced light and audio technology, the 3D likeness was startling, right down to his uneven dimples, his right deeper than his left, and his precise enunciation of consonants. This version of Matthew wore his favorite sweatpants with the sagging knees and the Cold Play concert tee nearly transparent from wear. She hadn't subscribed to the hologram service so she could complain about the little things, but here it was, conveniently. Her new job gave her no pleasure. Her coworkers were petty. She managed the office for a nonprofit that supported displaced artists while they worked on large-scale installations for the city of Miami. The executive director treated her like a personal assistant—without the perks of coffee and a business phone—and the woman constantly sighed with implied disappointment in Valerie's abilities.

"Take your issues to the board," Matthew's hologram said.

"I'm not going to be *that* employee."

"Fuck her."

Valerie took her eyes off her knife and regarded Matthew's hologram. His concerned expression looked frozen, as if there was a glitch in Wi-Fi. The real Matthew hadn't used profanity. She did, and often, but not him. Doing so would've meant he felt passionate about something.

"I'll try not to take things so personally," she said to change the subject.

"Tell the bitch to get off your back," the hologram continued. The pensive frown was replaced by a smile that made him appear as if he were trying to ace an interview. She made a mental note to contact the company. Little things mattered.

With the blade of her knife, she raked the diced onion into a bowl.

"Fuck her. Fuck her." The hologram grew fuzzier and with a startling pop, Matthew's image disappeared. Again.

HoloVision offered two levels of subscription. Valerie had chosen conversationally interactive, the most expensive level because she wanted more than to *see* Matthew. She had photos for that. There were things she felt she needed to say, matters left unresolved by his decision to end his life, and the service was an opportunity to do so in the privacy of her apartment. The monthly subscription was expensive but the payout from Matthew's life insurance had padded their joint savings considerably. Whether he'd intentionally waited until the company's exclusion period was over was unknown, but she suspected as much. He was methodical that way. In any case, money had never been an issue for them. Her parents had seen to that, the fact of which had been a source of angst for Matthew. He considered it cheating—as if to be an adult meant one had to suffer. For her, having money simply meant having choices. She signed a contract for the monthly hologram service which she could cancel at any time. The first day she turned it on and saw her Matthew standing before her, she was overcome with competing emotions and had to turn it off after only ten minutes. But she tried it again knowing Matthew would have appreciated its brilliance.

On her day off, Valerie Ubered to the HoloVision offices in Brickell. Her white Prius sat tucked away in its designated spot on her building's fifth-floor parking deck, and that's where it mostly stayed because work and Whole Foods were only a few blocks away and Miami drivers lived up to their reputation.

"You're not happy with the product," Keen said. Keen, the man to whom she was delivered by a stony-faced receptionist, sat behind a metal desk covered with clutter and regarded her. Dark eyes behind black-rimmed glasses dominated his face. Valerie sat across from him in a fussy wingback chair that didn't match the rest of the utilitarian office. An odor of bologna hung in the air.

She leaned forward, eager to be heard. "It's incredible! For the most part. But there are issues, yes."

He pushed his glasses further up his nose. "Such as?"

"Well, like the hologram swears a lot and my husband doesn't. *Didn't.*"

Keen turned to his computer and started typing. "Sometimes it takes some tweaking to get the personality just right from the information we're given."

The *personality*.

When Valerie had signed up, she had pages and pages of back history to fill out online. Facts about Matthew, his upbringing, beliefs, education, habits, common phrases, etc. Certainly swearing had been on the forms somewhere.

"Also, he wasn't one to go on and on about my looks. The hologram does a lot of gushing."

"You do realize the service has limitations?" Keen smiled and winced, as if to assure her it was an honest question and not a sarcastic dig.

"Of course. I thought… Your website says…"

"We'll definitely make it better for you. It's just that some people won't ever be satisfied because they're grieving, and well…we can't bring their loved ones back."

"This is only temporary," she said, her tone business-like. She wanted this guy to understand she knew reality from fantasy.

"I don't mean to offend," Keen said. Behind his hipster glasses, his eyes were sincere. "It's hard to lose someone you love."

Valerie nodded. She looked around the office, anywhere but at Keen as she didn't want to give in to tears, and her eyes settled on the row of Star Trek Bobble-Heads on top of a file cabinet.

"I'll have a revision streaming by the middle of next week," Keen said. "In the meantime, enjoy the compliments."

She declined his offer to show her out of the building.

The rain started a block away from Whole Foods. Rain showers were almost an everyday occurrence in Miami and yet she still hadn't bothered to buy an umbrella. Her phone vibrated in the pocket of her jeans. She ducked under the generous awning of a nearby bank and slipped it out.

Hey. Hru?

Ivan. She recognized his number. She'd deleted him from her contacts but hadn't blocked him. A part of her wanted to ignore his text, pretend she never saw it, pretend she *had* blocked him, but she also wanted to hear from him, wanted to feel loved, even if imperfectly, especially now, when she was feeling unlovable.

Good thanks for asking. U?
Waiting for you to come back
Don't
Come back, Val

It was tempting to return to New Hampshire, to everything she knew, to her best friend Kelly, to Ivan. There were moments after Matthew's suicide, she opened her computer to look at real estate in her old town only to close it again. Panic over the future was somehow easier than facing guilt and defeat.

There's nothing there for me
Ouch...

She'd met Ivan in a cooking class offered by their local community college. The same college where Matthew taught art history. Signing up gave her the kind of thrill she got when choosing a surprise gift. At the time, she was a terrible cook, but she imagined dazzling Matthew with a full-on French meal, imagined his look of appreciation when she presented elaborate dishes that took hours to make. Through her cooking she would love him out of his depression.

Ivan was tall and pasty white, all awkward limbs and a nose too large for his face. He'd given up plumbing for his dream of owning a small restaurant. After each class they took together, she found him more and more attractive. Every night he had the class doubled over with his self-deprecating humor and quirky way of seeing the world. He was completely new to the kitchen. Valerie asked him why he wanted to start a restaurant if he'd never cooked so much as an egg. To make people happy, he told her. She wondered if happy was a state Matthew would ever reach. They were married nine years by then and she'd become inured to his rough patches. That was a mistake, obviously. She was also mistaken in thinking that if she took care of her own loneliness, she'd be better able to help her husband through his.

How's your boy? Valerie texted.

After she and Matthew moved to Miami, Ivan returned to his ex and their four-year-old. Ivan and the boy's mother weren't married, had no intention to marry, and sometimes that meant they could easily retreat to a different place when their relationship got prickly.

Keeps me hopping on the daily

With Ivan she felt *seen*, but the only thing they ever did, really, was talk. There was the one time they kissed, a chaste and too-quick peck on the lips before they each got in their vehicles to drive home through a mesmerizing snowstorm. That was it. She enjoyed his friendship, enjoyed being able to be herself without worrying about saying the wrong thing. But Ivan wanted more, he made that clear from the start, and she was tempted, which was why after they moved to Miami, she had ignored his calls and texts. Until now.

Send me a pic
Of?
Where are you?
Walking to the market
Show me what's across the street from you rn

On the corner, Valerie spotted the strange little store she'd seen on her previous trek to Whole Foods. She crossed the street diagonally, causing a driver to blast his horn at her. In the storefront window, rubber masks hung on a display shelf, surrounded by old metal signs, plastic figurines, and comic books. She snapped a picture of Trump's face, drooping and distorted, and sent it to Ivan.

Did I ask for dog shit? Next time a sunset lol

Valerie sent a heart emoji and turned off her phone.

The nonprofit that employed Valerie was situated over a CVS, three blocks up the boulevard from her apartment. The paintings on the walls were the only indication that its mission was art-related as Ikea furnished the space and a drab gray carpet covered the floors. Even the view, in the offices afforded one, was of the building next door rather than the bay. Valerie could see the building's pool from her desk, but that scene grew dull with its daily parade of buff and tan bodies lounging in the sun.

"You were late this morning."

Her boss, Evie, peered into Valerie's office. Valerie was still trying to figure out why her boss was such a misery. Evie was an attractive but hard woman, with her dark slashes of eyeliner and violet colored lipstick, remnants from the eighties.

"I don't believe I was," Valerie said.

"We had a meeting with the artist from Connecticut via Skype."

"You'll need to invite me to the meetings you want me to attend."

Evie looked perplexed.

"I can show you how," Valerie offered.

"Assume *whenever* you see a meeting scheduled on the calendar, I want you to attend. Do I have to hold your hand, too?" Evie said, before moving on down the hall.

It took all of five minutes for Valerie to pack her laptop into her bag, write passwords on a sticky note for the desktop, and grab her purse and tote. On her way out, she let the receptionist know she wouldn't be back and to mail her last check.

That evening, Valerie had started preparing a Greek lemon chicken soup when her friend Kelly called to complain about the foot and a half of snow a Nor'easter had dumped. "Ask me to come play tourist for a week," she pleaded.

"Of course. Come!" She didn't tell Kelly she was newly free because she'd just quit her job. She didn't tell her she had no idea what she'd do next. What she wanted to be when she grew up was a question she had yet to answer since getting her degree in Art History. But like the hologram had said, Fuck Evie.

"You don't have to ask me twice!" Kelly said.

Valerie ate her soup standing in front of her window overlooking the bay. She enjoyed cooking, the sensuality of ingredients, the fragrant, smooth skin of a peeled garlic bulb, the tart aroma of a zested lemon. She'd started out wanting to create magic for Matthew, but the act of cooking only reminded her of Ivan. Matthew hadn't reacted the way she'd hoped anyway. The dish she made for him was steak and poutine, something his French-Canadian grandmother made on Sundays. He'd brought papers to the table to grade while he ate and Valerie watched him absent-mindedly bring fork to mouth while he ticked red marks on the students' work. "That was good," was all he said when he stood up from the table, papers in hand.

A fireworks display, one to rival any she'd seen back home in New Hampshire, lit the sky over a large yacht in the bay. Every day in Miami was a party for someone. An ambulance whined and weaved its way through the stopped traffic below. She thought of Matthew. His body, cold and still, must have been delivered by ambulance to the hospital after his student found him. She wondered why he chose his classroom over his home. She wondered if the siren had been wailing or silent.

"I quit my job today."

Matthew's hologram sat on the toilet lid while Valerie soaked in bubbles and shaved her calves. The hologram nodded and said, "It was a waste of your talents."

"I'm not sure what my talents are, exactly." Her Art History major had seemed like a good idea at the time, but she felt completely disconnected from it. She didn't want to be an academic like Matthew and she didn't want to work in a museum. "Evie reminded me of your mother. That same capacity to freeze a person out."

"My mother wasn't like that."

"She was ice cold. I wonder if that's why you turned inward so much."

"I was depressed. Chemical imbalance. It wasn't my mother who caused it."

Valerie added more hot water to her tepid bath, then agitated the remaining bubbles. One time after Mathew had come home from a visit with his mother, he told Valerie his mother had spent the whole time lecturing him about his career choice. It was beneath him, she'd said. After that visit he looked so tired, as if she'd drained the life from him. "Your mother was impossible. She used to constantly criticize you and it drove me mad. I had so much rage then, at your mother, at the situation, that I called her up and let her have it."

"How did that go?"

"She didn't speak to me for a month. Remember?" It had felt so good at the time to blame Matthew's mother for his depression, but it hadn't helped.

"You look so beautiful in this light, Valerie."

"My point in bringing this up is that I'm still angry at her, Matthew."

"Neurology. Not my mother."

This has never happened before, Keen said. He sat across from Valerie at a stained, rickety café table. She'd emailed him with her concerns, asking if it were possible to get a few more tweaks. She still hadn't said all she wanted to say to Matthew because the hologram was acting erratically. Sometimes, she'd turn it on and the hologram would talk to her like he was an actor in a porn movie. Other times, it would spit out irrelevant trivia.

"Well, I'm nearly done with the service anyway." At least, she *wants* to be done with it.

"You need friends here." Keen shoved half of a lemon bar into his mouth.

A steady stream of customers entered the café. Hot, humid air swirled its way inside each time the door opened.

"I have plenty of friends back home, you know." She could honestly only think of two: Kelly and Ivan. "Really fun friends."

"Yeah, but you're here. And who do you even know here? Your coworkers?"

Coworkers. Not anymore. They hadn't been friendly, anyway.

"I'm going to this party this weekend," Keen said. "You should come with me." He took a sip of his latte and wiped foam and lemon bar crumbs from his face.

"Are you hitting on me?" She was teasing him. "How old are you? Are you even old enough to drink?"

He gave her a mock-offended look. "I'm not asking you on a *date*. I'm helping you with your sad social life. Consider it an additional service, free of charge."

She should take him up on the offer. Other than his, she didn't know a friendly face in Miami. In the last week, there had been a couple of job interviews, but nothing that suited her. She was treading water here.

Keen picked at his cup holder. Shredded bits of cardboard lay on the table. "Some people who sign on for our hologram service don't have any options but to live in the past. They're usually older, missing a spouse. Occasionally we get a grieving parent. Those are tough. But you, you're young…ish." He gave her an apologetic smile and pushed his glasses up. "Don't tell my bosses that I said this, but you probably don't really need our service."

Valerie finished her latte. She smiled and stood, grabbing her empty cup and napkin. "Email me the address of the party. You never know." She already knew she wouldn't go. Recently widowed, jobless, no friends. What would she have to talk about?

Her Uber driver dropped her off on the corner. The restaurant, a vine-covered two-story building, sat along the river that flowed between Brickell and downtown Miami.

A hostess in a slinky black dress led her through the dining room. The restaurant was open on one side to the elements and the river. A gray barge floated past. The ad had said the owner was looking for an assistant in the kitchen and Valerie thought, why not? She followed the hostess up a set of spiral stairs to an office on the second floor.

Marisol, the owner, held her curly black hair off her face in a thick ponytail and wore a bandana tied around her forehead. She asked Valerie what kind of kitchen experience she had.

"None? But I took a class on French cuisine."

"Ai, ai, ai." Marisol clicked her tongue. "I need someone with experience. If not that then at least a culinary degree."

Feeling foolish, Valerie said she was sorry for wasting time and walked out of the office.

"Do you want to wash dishes?" Marisol called after her. "I have a spot in the pit open."

Valerie received a text from Ivan while she waited outside for her Uber to take her home.

Hru? When r u coming home?

I am home, she answered back, but it was a statement that didn't feel completely honest.

I want to see you

That phrase used to lift her spirits but also, at her loneliest, frustrate her as she knew she and Ivan could only ever be friends. But here she was reading them on her phone, and she no longer felt much of anything.

You're with someone else, Ivan

Opening a coffee shop. And sandwiches!

Congrats!

No fancy dishes from class. Lol! Come help me run it. You and I could live in the apartment above.

She started to respond but another text from Ivan arrived: *I want you, Val. For more than a friend. I want to live together and have a happy life.*

Returning to New Hampshire would feel wrong. Like going backward. Plus, she didn't want to be the kind of person who thinks nothing of breaking up a relationship. If it's meant to end, it will. She couldn't bring herself to respond right away. When she did, hours later, *I'm sorry* was all she sent.

Matthew's hologram sat in her reading chair next to the closet. Valerie stretched out on her bed and watched the changing colors light up the Freedom Tower outside her floor-to-ceiling window.

"Your depression made it difficult to know you, Matthew, to love you. Because how could I love you if you wouldn't let me know you?"

She'd first spotted him in the cafeteria line. He let her cut in front of him. He had great dimples and an open, friendly face. They kept running into each other in random places on campus and the following semester they were in the same Philosophy class.

She'd lost her parents almost a year apart from each other, first, her father and then her mother, and here was this quiet, gentle guy who ate lunch with her outside the library, who studied with her, who listened to her without judgment. Who, like her at the time, loved art and all the clues of history within. She believed he was her person. So, she said yes to marriage despite already seeing red flags. Winters were especially hard. His quiet became a fortress she could not breach. Occasionally he would explode in rage at some perceived criticism or judgment from her and just as quickly it would dissolve. In those hard months, he showed little interest in her beyond the pragmatic: What should I get for dinner? Did you pay the light bill? Would you mind running my shirts to the cleaners?

"You deserved more," Matthew's hologram said.

"I know and sometimes I hated you for it."

"I'm sorry."

"Two words I never heard from you. You focused on your own pain after we married. You hardly looked at me. You rarely spoke to me, even." Matthew's hologram looked more like her husband than ever. The barely-there expression on his face, the way the hologram looked away from her whenever she said something disagreeable. "I had a sort-of affair. An almost affair. And it felt wonderful! I was noticed and listened to!"

Matthew's hologram blinked.

"I chose *you* and you left me anyway!" Valerie bent at the waist and clutched her stomach. She was tired of crying. She moved off her bed and stood near the window. A line of brake lights like rubies lit up one lane of the boulevard below. The Freedom Tower turned yellow then red then violet. "There's a part of me that feels relief that you're gone, and I don't know how to deal with the awfulness of that fact," she said without looking at the hologram.

"You were a good wife."

"I was a shitty wife."

"You look so beautiful in this light, Valerie. I'd like to take you, right here, bend you right over."

A laugh-cry puffed out of her. She turned around to face the hologram image. "I guess I've said enough," she said, unplugging the machine. "Goodbye, Matthew."

Valerie found the kiosk at Bayside Park and bought a ticket. Kelly would be arriving in a week and Valerie wanted to give the Miami tour a test run. Someone was playing a clarinet further down in the park. The scent of popcorn wafted in the air close by and made her mouth water. Couples and families walked by her on their way to Bayside Park. Valerie had started taking in how colorful and vibrant the city was, especially at night when buildings and boats and sometimes even the cars were lit in pastels and neon. She and Matthew had only seen the downtown area where they lived. She'd tried to get him out to see the graffiti in Wynwood or the cool architecture in the Design District, but he was always too tired. After the work of unpacking was over, most evenings he sat in front of the television watching the news or mind-numbing police dramas.

The ticket seller told Valerie she could get off at any of the five stops and explore or she could stay on for the entire loop and start again. She chose a seat at the top of the bus, near the front. On the other side of the road, a flock of hens, vibrantly hued, pecked the grass, unfazed by cars and pedestrians. The sun warmed her shoulders. She took out a tube of sunscreen from her bag and rubbed it into her exposed skin. Valerie wasn't certain about staying in Miami. She only knew she didn't want to move back to what was familiar and safe. If she returned to New Hampshire, to Ivan, her life would shrink, not expand.

A young tour guide bounded up the stairs to his place at the front and started bantering into the mic. Valerie fanned herself with her hat.

The bus lurched forward.

IN THESE DARK WOODS

The woman has walked this path circling the reservoir many times. She stays in a simple but sturdy cabin near the base of the mountain when she's up from the city. When she pulled into the parking lot off the highway, there was only one other vehicle: a white truck. To get to the head of the path, she had to hike uphill for a mile and a half. The dirt road winding around the lake will be another mile. She likes to walk up here to clear her mind, to make space in her head for inspiration, for creativity to grace her or give her the finger whichever it's inclined to do.

In summer, families might share the path or swim in the clear cold spring-fed water. People who, like her, prefer to go out of their way for whatever small patches of pure and untouched parts of nature still exist. Today, clouds hang low and gauze-like. Thunder growls beyond her line of vision. There is no one swimming. No families or couples spread out on blankets. There is just her and the mountain and the lake and the head of the path before her.

The woman is famous; first, for being an artist, and second for being a feminist. She began with conceptual art: short films, small performance studies, still-lifes that relied on the absurd. Her recent *Soul of a Woman* series has made her something of a celebrity. Each piece is a wall-sized collage using mixed media and found objects. The woman interviews other women, sometimes for days, sometimes weeks, gathering what she calls the tangible material of the intangible.

It is the end of August. A time in which the city has grown hot and irritable and this area in Vermont already holds the promise of apple cider and pumpkins. It'll be the last time she'll walk this path before spring. Her cabin isn't built for winter. Now, near the top of this small mountain, the air is cool and smells of fish. There is little bird song. No high-pitched calls from tree swallows. No chatter from goldfinches. Only the crows still heckle from the tops of trees. The sweet scent of pine is thick in the damp, cool air. The woman takes note of the flowers decorating the sides of the path as she passes, one sneakered foot in front of the other: white clover, Queen Anne's lace, black-eyed Susans, daisies, and pale purple asters. Flowers that dotted her childhood summer days. And deeper in the woods, earlier in the summer, there were striped trilliums and pink lady slippers. In the meadows, bluets and buttercups, Indian paintbrushes and golden rod.

Above the woman's head, the pine branches rustle and shimmer in the breeze, a soothing susurrus.

In a recent article, a critic who writes for *Art Today* stated that the woman's vision is important. "Viewed individually and as a whole, this body of work forces the viewer to see a woman beyond social norms. Each woman is as varied and complicated as a universe. Each piece tells the story of a life lived awake and with feeling. No longer will women stand for being reduced or invisible the work seems to say."

Last month, on this very path, the woman plucked red raspberries, small explosions of sweet and tart on her tongue. Now, the berries appear shriveled and ravaged by birds or bears or people. The bushes hold only those still green and sour and likely to never ripen.

She's not quite halfway around the lake when she hears the patter of rain falling on the trees above her, like dog paws on a wooden floor. To her left, light shimmers on the metal-gray of the lake. Rotted and naked logs lie like fallen soldiers along its bank.

Hair rises on her arms. A feeling of being watched. The woods have always been safe for her. Even as young as eight, she explored the forest near her house. This day, though, she can't shake her uneasiness. She peers through the trees on either side, past clutches of birch and firs. Through brush and shrubbery too thick. The feeling reminds her of the story her lover told her about being in Canada on an assignment and how it felt to be stalked by a polar bear. To know that even when you can't see them, there's at least one eyeing you for dinner. "They're cannibals," her lover had said. "They'll eat their own kids." He told her he had nightmares about being mauled by one for years after that assignment. "The only animals known to intentionally hunt humans," he said, his voice low and heavy with awe.

A drop of rain taps her cheek and takes her out of her fear. No one would be out in weather like this. Plus, she's already been raped. Her freshman year of college. Now that she's older, *much* older, two acts of sexual violence in one lifetime are unlikely. Since turning forty, she's told herself this.

Her lover died last November on assignment. He was writing a piece on how Yemen still promoted tourism amidst instability. He sent her pictures of dragon's blood trees and sap that flowed red—red like his own blood lost when an airstrike hit his hotel. She misses him. Misses texting him randomly or sending him pictures of weird things. Misses his strong body, easy smile, and skilled tongue. No man made her orgasm like he did. Sometimes she thinks he can still see her from wherever he is or isn't. Sometimes she believes he might now be privy to her thoughts. She hopes so. She hopes he feels duly appreciated and even a little shocked. He was a bit of a prude for all his worldliness. They had a weekend in Paris—he flew her there to meet him—and their first night he asked her why she was so vulgar. They were in bed. With the curtains open, they could see into the Catholic school across the alleyway. School was out for Christmas break.

"You don't like the word fuck when we're fucking." She'd rolled her eyes but his eyes were on the ceiling.

"You talk like a man."

"I talk like a woman having a good time."

"You talk like a porn star."

"Maybe I like porn."

"You can't be a feminist and like porn."

"Fuck you. Then when you're finished, fuck me."

They ended up laughing about it, but after that weekend, she became self-conscious about what came out of her mouth during sex. She wishes now she hadn't conceded so easily.

A horse fly careens through the air around the woman's face. She bats at it with her hand and makes contact. Steps on its stunned body as she passes.

She's more than halfway around the reservoir. Here is the old stone wall built by settling farmers two hundred years earlier. Here is the crumbling foundation of an old standing well further on. The woman checks the sky when she hears thunder but there's been no rain since the drop on her face, though the air has thickened. Crickets sound off in distant meadows.

The woman wants to interview a writer, a friend of her lover, whom she met at his memorial service. The writer has traveled all over the world. Most recently, Jakarta. The writer flew there to escort her elderly Indonesian friend on a Hajj trip to Saudi Arabia. Not allowed to leave her hotel room in Medina because she wasn't a Muslim, the writer hung out in the hotel, which she said was like a small city anyway.

As she walks, the woman's mind shifts to what she might include in a collage of her own life: Eiffel Tower, details from a Kandinsky, a brown bear in a window, black-eyed Susans, a picture of Vincent Price, a rust bloom on a pipeline, a positive pregnancy test.

A bird flies up from a cluster of bushes and startles the woman. She jumps and lets out a quiet, "Oh."

A figure emerges around the corner further down the path.

The woman is newly alert, maybe even alarmed, though she knew in the back of her mind she wasn't alone on this mountain path near the lake. She remembers the truck. Never forgot it, really.

As the figure approaches, the woman sees it is a man. He is tall and large, but not muscular. The man, bald, wears maroon running pants which bag at the knee and a dark blue tee, wet under the arms and against his stomach. She's close enough to smell him: body odor, a hint of beer, a hint of rot, and under these animal smells, the perfume of dryer sheets.

She tries to catch his eye before she passes but he doesn't look at her. He looks ahead, as if she doesn't exist, as if she's not walking on the same path around the lake in the woods as he. Hair rises on her arms.

She's almost back to the point where she started, the place where the path ends and the gravel road begins. He's going the opposite way and for this she feels relief.

She walks a few steps before she looks behind her.

The woman sees the man has also stopped. He's looking up at something in the trees. Her palms grow slick with sweat. The man lowers his gaze to settle on her, then starts moving toward her.

Her lover told her that to have even the slimmest chance of surviving an encounter with a polar bear you must avoid acting like prey. "They'll smell your fear," he said. "You can't outrun them. You can't out fight them. Playing dead only makes things easy for them. Might as well stand there and imagine white light or pray or use whatever other magic tricks you've come to rely on."

An end of summer day. A clear, cold lake at the top of a small mountain. A gray sky that threatens.

Here is the woman. Here is her light.

ACKNOWLEDGMENTS

Many thanks to Angela Mitchell, Gordon Krupsky, Becky Hagenston, and Kim Chinquee, editors of the journals in which these stories first appeared in slightly different forms:

"Burner," *Nelle*
"Here In The Jungle," *Slippery Elm*
"You Look So Beautiful In This Light," *The MacGuffin*
"Tell Me What To Do," *Jabberwock Review*
"In These Dark Woods," *New World Writing Quarterly*

A special thank you to Louise Marburg, my first reader, inspiring writing partner, and dear friend. Thank you for being so funny—in your fabulous stories and in life—and thank you for championing this book and keeping me on task.

My sincere gratitude, also, to talented writers Megan Mayhew-Bergman, Cliff Garstang, Jill McCorkle and David James Poissant, for their generosity and words of support. Thank you to the following writers for their keen insight and editorial feedback on some or all of these stories: Kris Fatz, Shannon Cain, and Doug Silver. A heartfelt thank you to Christine Butterworth McDermott and John McDermott, former editors of *REAL: Regarding Arts & Letters* for their belief in my work over the years.

Thank you to Cornerstone Press: Dr. Ross Tangedal, director and publisher; Paige Biever, managing editor; Allison

Lange, cover designer; and the rest of the amazing editorial and production team.

Many of these stories were drafted and/or revised while in residence at the Virginia Center for the Creative Arts, Vermont Studio Center, and Weymouth Center for the Arts & Humanities. My sincere thanks to these special places and to the people whose dedication and hard work keep them open.

Thank you to these inspiring teachers: Richard Bausch, Stacy D'Erasmo, Christine Schutt, the late Kevin McIlvoy (Mc), and the late Alan Wier.

My mother and father, both book lovers, lit the fire of reading in me and for that, and many other things, I will forever be grateful. Thank you to Susan Grimaldi, the *real deal,* for her heart and wisdom. And to Damita Nocton, thank you for being the best literary friend a person could have.

My profound thanks to my sons David and Alexander for all the joy, life lessons, and for being such good men. And lastly, I cannot adequately express the amount of gratitude I have for my husband, for his steadfast love, his belief in me, and without whom this book would not exist. Tom, you are the foundation and the magic.

**Author's Note: The art installation in the story "Tell Me What to Do," is real. It's* Untitled (Eels) *by Patty Chang.*

Katrina Denza's stories have appeared in *Confrontation, Emerson Review, Jabberwock Review, Nelle, New Delta Review, New World Writing, Passages North, REAL: Regarding Arts & Letters*, and *The MacGuffin*, among other places. She is the recipient of a scholarship from the Bread Loaf Writers' Conference and a fellowship from the Virginia Center for the Creative Arts. She resides in North Carolina with her husband.